Branches

by Jessica Dailey
and Casey Robert Swanson

Branches

By Jessica Dailey and Casey Robert Swanson

ISBN # 979-8-9986992-6-9
eISBN # 979-8-9986992-7-6

This is a work of future fiction. Any resemblance to people, places and incidents is purely coincidental.

Copyright 2025, Casey Swanson, Jessica Dailey
All Rights Reserved

Dedication

This book is dedicated to our parents; Robert H Dailey and Alice Dailey, Earl C Swanson and Margaret Swanson without whose guidance and support we never would have taken up the written word and whose love we will never forget.

Chapter 1

The Surface of the planet she approached with her apprentice in their long-range craft was more barren than she had expected from her observations from the small orbiting station feeds.

This small orbiting station (small by the standards of the Explorer's Guild) had a docking bay for the explorers two-person long-rang craft and a second docking bay for resupply missions. The interior had just three modules at the time of their arrival; control, living and supply. More modules would come later as the exploration of the planet developed. Those satellites she had worked from in the past also had contained a module for the explorers work.

This was her first First Landing Mission. Just the thought of being the first to explore this new world had been the ultimate achievement she had worked so hard for. These First Landing missions only went to Senior Explorers with at least three missions under them. They were rare to get and based on the ratings points she had achieved on her previous missions, both as apprentice and explorer. This was her seventh mission now, the third with Sulligan as her apprentice.

The video Feed came back showing that a civilization had been here once. Portions of the remains could be seen from the orbiting station. That was a long time ago, before some unknown force, some catastrophe, had stripped the planet of its water and most of its atmosphere. They would mostly be using the air they brought with them on the mission. Technology had improved since the first missions of exploration by the Guild. Scientist had discovered a different manner to store Oxygen so as to ensure there would be more then enough for the two of them, giving them the time to explore the planet. There would always small amounts of oxygen that was lost to leakage and they still had to maintain a careful balance between air, water and unrecoverable waste.

There was a beauty in these lost worlds that kept her alive. Their vast emptiness carried their own significance to her. A feeling of great discovery of the mysteries of what happened on these worlds stirred an excitement within her that kept her mind going. Just thinking about what was ahead of her and Sulligan kept her mind racing to what awaited them. That was something her husband, Gustof, had a hard time understanding. They were married three years now. He was two years older than her and to Gustof the universe beyond their home planet was just an empty thing.

~ ~ ~ ~ ~

As Sulligan was working on the technical side of things, she remembered her last conversation with her husband Gustof before she had left for this mission. Gustof stood at six foot one with broad shoulders from his daily swimming. He had short, sandy hair with green eyes. He had not shaven so he had a full day's beard growth on his face. She was five foot eight with light brown eyes and light brunette hair. She was slim and very fit due to her intense training as part of the Exploration Guild. She loved when he had a little rugged look to him like today.

Gustof spoke to her in a soft voice.

"We have a good life here, Anya. You are highly respected in your field, you made Senior Explorer a year early, I am so proud of your achievements. But why do you put your life in danger, mission after mission. Six months away at a time is a long time. This mission came up so quickly that we have not even had time to recover from your last mission. We had agreed on more time together after that last mission. You could be here with me in our home, with the living beauty of nature all around us."

Gustof tried to understand the limited time in space, exploring, that she had. However weren't six missions in ten years and her dedication to the Guild enough.

Anya could only look at him as they sat on the bank of the creek near their home. Her fishing pole lay beside her. Gustof's line was in the water, its lure searching for the proper size rainbow trout he had programmed it for; over 12 inches but under 18 inches in length. As Anya looked at him he seemed so at peace with her. There was a connection beyond the physical that existed between the two of them. How could he begin to understand how powerless she felt amongst so much life?

Gustof looked over at Anya, sitting on the bank next to him. She didn't enjoy fishing like he did, but she always came fishing with him when she was earthbound. The tranquility of it brought them closer together.

She knew Gustof was right; they needed to be together more than they had been. She turned to Gustof, speaking as she looked into his eyes.

"Gustof I love you with all my being and you know that. But you also know that this is part of what I am, because in this line of work your space career is short lived. And when the opportunity comes you have to take it. I will never get this one again. You are my anchor, Gustof, someone for me to hold onto in my thoughts when I am in space. You are all that I think of and have ever wanted. I love our life here on the farm and watching you working, making your discoveries. It makes me so happy for you. And I watch as you create new ways for the missions to survive. We fit so well together and we need each other.

"I only have three more years," she said to Gustav.

Gustof looked in her beautiful light brown eyes, reached out and held her hand close to him.

"I know what I signed up for when we married; it is just sometimes I miss you so much it hurts. And I have started to worry about you even more, I don't know why?"

"Gustof," she replied, "I have trained for this my entire life. I know what I am doing up there, I have always returned to you and always will. I am safer up there than I am crossing the street down here. Please do not worry so much about me."

"Will Sully be your apprentice again?" Gustof asked her. He liked the guy and they quickly become friends. He knew and trusted the both of them. He had to; they would be spending six months alone together on their missions. A closeness between Anya and Sully was to be expected. Senior explores and their apprentices were matched with this in mind.

There had been two disasters early in the program between mismatched people. People who could not, even with all their training, work together as one unit; understanding what the other person is doing; the ability take orders without question from each other; and to see what their exploration partner was thinking. Now the Explorer and apprentice were matched as much through psychological as physical training. Closeness was built up between the two explorers based in part on their compatibility. A computer program that the Explorers 'Guild had developed was designed to do just that.

~ ~ ~ ~ ~

Sulligan looked over at his Senior Explorer, his commander in these missions and his friend in life. She was sitting now intently at the controls, watching the readings as the shuttle approached the planets surface not far from what she had identified from space as a significant ruin. A closeness had built up between the two explorers based in part on their compatibility and that was to be expected. However there was a growing closeness from the excitement they shared with space and their discoveries they made together. A bond of friendship had formed beyond what was expected and this allowed them to work together almost as one. It was this bond that had played a huge part in her promotion to Senior Explorer. The bond that formed so naturally between the two was something a program could not recreate.

As Sulligan looked over at his Senior Explorer, he thought of the special relationship she had with her husband, Gustof. He wondered if he would ever have in his own life a relationship with the strength he saw in theirs. Who would be his bedrock, whom he could trust as Anya and Gustof trusted each other.

The planet was fast approaching and Sulligan went back to his duties. He pushed to the background the mild jealousy he felt at times regarding Anya and Gustof and their shared life together.

Sulligan's voice broke into Anya's thoughts and he looked over to his leader with a broad smile on his face and excitement in his eyes.

"Even less atmosphere than thought, that's not good,' Sulligan said to Anya. 'We will be almost totally dependent on the air supply we have brought with us."

Anya looked over at Sulligan.

"We should be fine. With the improvements the Guild has made in our air regeneration systems, there will be plenty of air for us as we explore the planet."

"I just wanted you to be made aware of the thin atmosphere we'll be in," Sulligan told his commander.

Anya now returned Sulligan's smile and spoke to him.

"Can you believe it, we're here" she said with energy in her voice.

Sulligan replied, "I am so happy right now; I can't explain what I am feeling but it's good. My heart is pounding in my chest this is just unbelievable."

"I know exactly how you feel," Anya responded.

~ ~ ~ ~ ~

Gustof sat on his front porch with his two dogs at his feet. Gustof's mind drifted to his wife. He looked up at the stars, clearly visible in the warm fall night. She was up there, somewhere, exploring the universe. Anya had tried to show him with the large telescope on the porch she bought him where they were going. She was about to land on an unknown world, a First Landing, and he was so proud of what Anya had accomplished.

He thought of their time together when she was planet bound. There was never enough. She was always busy, reporting on the last mission or getting ready for the next. The time they did spend together was everything he wanted in life. But sometimes it just wasn't enough. "Her anchor," she called him, but where was his anchor.

Gustof knew she wanted to spend more time with him. In his heart he knew that they were destined to be as one. He remembered a conversation they had before she left on her first First Landing mission as an apprentice.

They had walked through his farm to a wooded area close by with his dogs. Anya had seen the huge oak tree from a distance and together they sat down beneath it.

As they sat down beneath the sprawling branches of the tree, Anya began to speak.

"You know Gustof; we are just like this magnificent Oak tree."

"What do you mean, Anya?"

"We started out together like this tree's roots, separate, but we came together as this trees trunk, strong and vibrant. As we have grown, we have worked in separate fields, branches of that trunk. And as this tree grows, its branches come together again in its crown. So we start to come together again as we grow. That is how I see us."

Gustof just looked over at Anya, overwhelmed by her love for him.

Anya smiled at Gustof and giggled.

"And someday, Mr. and Mrs. Branch will have lots of little acorns growing from it."

The just looked at each other and started laughing, that one moment in time would be always with them. They were Mr. and Mrs. Branch from that day onward through time itself. And nobody else would ever be let into that private little space.

Chapter 2

"Even less oxygen than we thought, that isn't good," Anya said aloud as she looked over the Shuttles atmospheric readings. "We will be almost totally dependent on the oxygen supply we bring with us."

They approached the expected landing site on the shuttles retractable wings. They could literally glide for miles, even on a planet with a limited atmosphere like here, to find the most optimal site for a landing; flat, without mounds, rocks or crevices more than a few inches in size. Their goal was to find a location as near as possible to the ruins they had spotted from the satellite. They could then begin their exploration of the planet immediately. Their time on the planet was limited.

It was up to the Anya to pick the final landing spot for the craft. The directions from the Guild were minimal on her initial site selection. Other explorers would follow her and expand the range of the exploration of this planet from what she would choose as the final base of operations for the two of them.

First Landing; this was the initial job that would set up all other future missions to this planet. This planet had been selected primarily through long-range scans from the home world. It fit a unique set of criteria that showed it had the capability to support life and was rich in the mineral wealth the Guild needed to continue its explorations of space. The Explorer's Guild placed an orbiting station in high orbit through robotic stasis. This satellite then relayed more information about the planet back to their home world. From this very limited information, the Guild chose to make this planet a priority target

After the initial scans from the orbiting station were received and confirmed the long range scans of the planet, two more modules were sent to join the orbiting station to prepare for the First Landing by a Senior Explorer. The first three modules would be enough for the First Landing as the Senior Explorer and their apprentice were expected to spend the entire three and a half month mission on the planet's surface. Two future modules would then be sent upon the return of the First Landing crew based on their reports and a decision to expand the exploration of the target planet.

Sulligan glanced in admiration as Anya worked the controls, keeping the shuttle airborne for as long as possible on its glide path as they watched the reports come in on the planet's surface. Her first guess as to a landing spot had proven to be too rocky, but she spotted another potential site even closer to the ruins.

The two of them, Senior Explorer and apprentice exchanged quick smiles at each other. Neither lacked any confidence in the skills and abilities of the other. Before they had landed on established bases and then given their assignment from the base. But this time there were no assignments, no direct orders from the Guild. Just three and a half months to explore a planet and in the end, before they left, establish the position of the future base from which all other missions on this planet would launch. This was central to the exploration philosophy of the Guild. The First Landing would choose the base site and future missions would spread out like a spider's web from that site.

Anya spotted a suitable landing site and her hands began to fly across the controls like a virtuoso playing her instrument. Early First Landings had been done by an auto-pilot and the computer on board the shuttle. These early missions had some near disasters because of that. Now all First Landing were done manually by the Senior Explorer. Piloting a shuttle was considered one of the chief skills necessary to become a Senior Explorer.

The site was not quite in their line of flight; she made the adjustment easily. Sulligan used his own controls in perfect symphony with hers. Their bond, the meshing of the physical and the intellect was almost perfect; a single combined being bringing the shuttle in to land.

The Wheels extruded from the belly of the shuttle, sixteen of them in four rows, and the shuttle touched down. The shuttle's speed still remained high. There was no room for a thing as mundane as a parachute to slow them down. Break usage would have to be minimal as well until the speed had deceased considerably. It was up to the skill of the pilot to guide the path of the shuttle until it stopped. A slight mound, almost invisible until the last moment, caught a set of the wheels, causing the shuttle to dip precariously to one side. A wing tip came within inches of touching the sandy surface. Almost to the ground, Anya's skill righted the shuttle with a skillful turn; once again all sixteen wheels on the ground. If the wing tip had touched it could have been disaster. A broken tip would have meant, in the best case, a reduced ability to explore the world and probably a slight loss of valuable air and water. Worst case, as had happened several times on First Landings, the shuttle would go pin-wheeling over it's stubby wings, wrecking the shuttle, destroying their valuable air and water supplies. Even if the two were to survive the crash, their time would be limited to hours, not even days, of life.

The communication between a First Landing and the Guild was limited. That would come later with an established base. The First Landing more closely approximated the first exploration ships sailing Earths oceans a thousand years before. The Guild would only find out the results of their mission upon their return. And if lost, they weren't even expected to return for another three and a half months. By then it would be too late for the First Landing explorers. The importance of judgment and sobriety on First Landing missions could not be underplayed. Only their very best teams could be expected to be successful, and even a few of those were lost.

The shuttle came to a full stop not one hundred yards from the ruins. The look the two explorers exchanged said it all: excitement, exultation and relief. Sulligan briefly clasped his commander's hand and squeezed.

"You did it," he said as he unclasped his belts, releasing him from his seat, and he rose to stand.

"We both did," she smiled back at him as she prepared to stand up as well. She pressed a button and the wings of the shuttle extended up and retracted. The shuttle for their purposes now was a sixteen-wheeled exploratory vehicle for surface exploration. And their living quarters for their time on the planet.

As the two got up and stretched themselves, relieving the tension in their muscles from the landing, they couldn't help but give each other a high five. Their closeness was apparent. It had to be for them to be successful. Their First, First landing was a success. Very few would be given the opportunity they were given here.

~ ~ ~ ~ ~

Gustof looked up from his seat in the combine (clear/plow/prepare/seed) tractor and stopped its forward movement. He had planted almost 20 acres of soy since early morning when he started the day. This was a soy variant he had helped to create for the Guild. In his greenhouse he was developing a another new variant that he hoped would increase the nutritional value of the soy and make it a more complete protein for the explorers and colonist of the Guild.

He looked at his watch and wrote down the time; 11:47 a.m. central planet time. She would confirm the time upon her return to Earth. The planet landing, her First Landing, it was a success. He sensed it instinctively, a result of their bond. He looked up into the heavens and smiled at her. His pride in her achievement was evident in the look on his face. Gustof recalled a fond memory of a dinner they had. The soft glow of candlelight danced on the table as they sat across from each other. Their hands intertwined and how beautiful she looked with her hair framing her face and those eyes that had melted his heart. They shared stories and laughed. He felt that night such contentment and love, he cherished that memory as it held her close to his heart.

He turned his tractor to automatic and stepped out of it. The combine would finish the planting overnight. The tractor/combine could do all of the work for him, however, that didn't feel like real farming to him and he tried to work the machines manually at least a few hours everyday. He walked home, cleaned up in the auto-shower in their home from his day in the fields, prepared a quick meal for himself and his two dogs and then sat on the front porch with them at his feet. That was his life when she was gone in space, working alone on his experimental Agg farm and alone on the porch but for his dogs.

~ ~ ~ ~ ~

"Atmosphere readings, Sulligan, is it as bad as we feared."

"Maybe worse, too limited for any exploration without suits, how did the Guild miss that?"

"Long range recon satellites contain very little information. It is mostly conjecture based on past experience with previous planets the Guild has reached."

"Do you think that we will ever find a living planet," Sulligan asked Anya as they looked out the shuttles front windows. "Every planet that the Guild has found so far has been a long dead one. We can't be alone, can we?" Sulligan sounded almost melancholy as he said that. For every explorer their greatest wish was to be the first to find a living culture.

The Senior Explorer looked inward before answering Sulligan's thought. Over one hundred planets now explored by the Guild. Over half had been found with long dead civilizations, like this. 'What had happened out here?' she thought to herself. Almost all of these lost civilizations perished around the same time. She had heard unconfirmed rumors in the Guild's Headquarters. She kept those to herself. She still believed there was a chance she would find life on another world or she wouldn't be an explorer.

"It's getting late," she answered Sulligan, intentionally ignoring his rhetorical question. "Let's shut down all of the flight systems and deploy the Solar Sail. We can start collecting energy before nightfall and conserve our resources that way."

It took only moments for Sulligan to deploy the sail from its compartment on the top of the shuttle. Fully deployed in sunlight, it would provide all of their energy needs during the exploration of the planet. At night they would run on the energy their batteries stored from the sail's energy conversion. The shuttle's insulation protected it from extreme temperatures and little energy was required to maintain a comfortable climate inside.

While Sulligan deployed the sail, Anya she shut down the remaining flight controls. They would not need those again until it was time to leave the planet. Only the radar remained active.

Both finished, she looked over at Sulligan.

"We'll rest until morning and begin our charting and exploration early." She smiled at Sulligan as she said this. Over the next three months the two would spend all of their time together exploring the planet. No directives or orders from the Guild, just point the shuttle whichever way they liked and see what lay over the next horizon.

Sulligan broke out his deck of cards and cribbage board.

"I'm up 150 points, loser prepares dinner tonight.

"Dinner?" she laughed as she sat down at the small table opposite him. 'You mean which meals to pop into the nuker for tonight's meal? You're on and this time no cheating."

"Cheating, me?" he laughed as he dealt the cards.

~ ~ ~ ~ ~

It was early afternoon, while sitting on a chair on his porch, when Gustof saw the dust coming up from the long road leading to his farm. Unlike most of his neighbors, he had never had his long private road paved over in the plexi-material most roads were paved over with now. "Keeps me closer to the earth," he'd tell people who asked him about that.

Gustof had very few visitors when Anya was not there; she was the social one. Except for heading into the local co-op store for his weekly supply runs or visiting the local pub, he seldom left the farm.

"Who could that be?" Gustof asked his dogs who were resting at his feet. They just looked up at him.

As the vehicle got closer, one of the new hydrogen-powered sports cars, Gustof got up from his chair on the porch and walked down to the driveway where the road ended next to the house.

The car pulled up and a tall man, wearing a beard and the latest men's fashion, climbed out.

"Gustof, old friend, It's been ages since I last saw you. Not since we both graduated from the Agg Guild University."

It was Stefen, an old college buddy from his student days with the Guild. They had hung out together at the pub and Gustaf had introduced him to many of his friends.

'What brought him here,' Gustof thought.

As if answering Gustof's thoughts Stefen continued what he was saying.

"I was visiting a farm just down the way from yours, following up on some Guild research, when they mentioned your farm here. I couldn't believe it. It's been years."

"Its nice to see you Stefen, it has been awhile. Come inside and don't mind the dogs. They're friendly."

Stefen knelt down before the two dogs and let them smell him. The he scratched each of them behind the ear before standing up.

"Do you have any ale inside, I'm parched."

"In the frig, come on inside and I'll get you one."

After they came into the house together, Stefen walked over to a mantle across from the entry way door as Gustof went to get the drinks. Stefen reached over to pick something up with one hand as he started to place the other hand on the mantle. The dogs barked and

Stefen put the second hand back into his pocket while he held a picture with his free hand.

As Gustof came back into the room he saw Stefen with the picture in his hand.

"The dogs don't like people touching Anya's things while she's away." Gustof said.

"Anya, your wife, a Senior Explorer I understand. She has quite a list of accomplishments. Is this from one of her missions?"

"Yes," answered Gustof, motioning to a place for Stefen to sit. The dogs lay between the two men, keeping an eye on Stefen.

"I understand she made Senior Explorer a year early. That was in all the news at the Guild. You must be proud of her."

"Yes I am very proud of her. What are you doing with yourself these days?" Gustof asked Stefen while they each took a drink from their ales.

"I am strictly doing statistical research now. Never could get a grasp on the actual farming side of the Guild. I understand you got that big research grant from the Explorer's Guild. At least that's what the guys back at the Agg Guild said."

"Yeah," answered Gustof, "I can't go into it, but it's a big thing."

"Have you heard from Michael or Tanya lately? You three used to be close."

"Tanya moved off planet and joined a Guild colony. Anya was able to help her with getting that. Tanya actually apprenticed on one trip with Anya before she got her current apprentice, Sulligan."

"Sulligan, whose that? I don't recognize the name."

"He is from the Explorer's Guild and wants to get involved with off-world archeology. This is their third mission together."

"Don't you worry about that, six months alone together? That would drive me crazy with jealousy."

"Not at all, all three of us are friends."

"What about Michael," Stefen asked.

"I see him every once in awhile. He's now the manager at the local Guild research lab here and we both frequent the same pub."

"Wow, that's great for him. Have you heard from any of the others lately?"

"Not really, Eric and Lewis moved off-world. Paul is in Paris. Masi is around some where's but I haven't talked to him in ages."

"Wow, three of us went off-world. I could never do that myself."

"I know what you mean, farming, the dirt, is enough for me," Gustof said.

"I have to go now; I have a Guild call to take. Can I see you again next week?" Stefen asked as he got up to leave.

"Sure," answered Gustof, not sure what else to say.

"Maybe you can show me your farm then?"

"Yes, that would be nice," answered Gustof as they got up from their chairs and went to the door. The research farm was something he was very proud of.

"Until then," Stefen called back to Gustof as he got into his car and sped off down the road.

Chapter 3

They rose early morning, Central Earth Time. Anya had lost the cribbage match the night before and it had been her job to prepare their evening meal; Turkey with Stuffing and a cream cake for desert. It was important to maintain their calorie count on these missions. Now it was Sulligan's turn to prepare the meal. The explorer's meals had come a long ways since that first mission launched a little more than 50 years earlier. And they still had a long ways to go to match fresh food. At least they were nutritious and didn't taste bad. Each expedition was able to choose their own meal plan. Today's meal, per the schedule, was french toast with freeze dried peaches, soy protein sausage (flavored with maple syrup it said, though neither could taste any of that) and coffee. At least that was fresh. Each Senior Explorer was given an allowance for a special food to take along. Anya had chosen 100 pounds of green coffee beans from West Africa. Their equipment roasted the bean and brewed a large mug of the coffee in about ten minutes. Her apprentice was also given a smaller allowance; he spent that on popcorn. Over breakfast, they discussed the mission ahead. However, before they got started with that Sulligan had a much more important matter to bring up.

"Anya, how is Gustof coming with his soybean research. I'm not sure how much more of this soy protein they give us I can eat."

"Thanks for asking. That grant the Guild gave him seems to have led to a breakthrough in quality and flavor. He just planted his latest Soy variation in the greenhouses when I left."

"Gustof took me in there the last time I visited. He seems pretty proud of his work. But the smell..."

"Yeah, I know, my husband," she said with a bit of irony, "only uses his own greenhouse fertilizer he produces on the farm. I've gotten used to it helping him in there, but still...it takes some getting used to."

They both laughed at that.

"Back to the job at hand," Anya began again. "It looks pretty good at this site for your work."

"It does, I can't wait to begin at the site. It looks like it will be mostly charting from the shuttle," Sulligan said between bites of food, the large mug of coffee in one hand. He didn't relish the coffee like she did, but it sure was a good way to start each day.

"If we see something significant we will use the suits," the Anya said in reply. "Some air loss is inevitable when using them. We'll have to be careful with that. This limited atmosphere will affect the trip."

"The airlocks only then," Sulligan responded. "Cumbersome and only one of us at a time, but at least we won't lose as much air that way."

"Exactly," Anya smiled.

"It pretty much eliminates the drones for air surveillance," Sulligan replied to her before taking a draught from his mug of the hot coffee. "I tried to launch one when I got up. Give us an aerial view of the nearby ruins. Not enough atmosphere to support it." They could both see though the side portal by the table the drone lying on the ground just a few feet from its launch port on the side of the shuttle.

"We'll pick it back up and put it back in its launcher," Anya said, looking at the drone sitting on the ground. "Then we'll see what those ruins have to offer."

"Great, I can't wait to see them up close. I've studied a lot of the ruins the Guild has found on other planets. I'll see how they compare," Sulligan answered back. His first love was off-planet archeology, what had driven him to join the Explorers Guild out of University.

"Then its horizon to horizon," she said to Sulligan. "I do not expect too many surprises on this trip. I think we will save the jet-drone for something unusual. We only have six hours of flight with it and I would like to get at least two missions out of the drone."

"That makes sense. Have you heard anything about the new shuttle designs? I hear that they'll have a greater drone capacity."

"That would be the Engineering Guild. They are working with our Guild on a innovative design, but I don't think its close yet."

"It would sure be nice to get an early shot at one of those when they're ready."

"Yes, it would. I am still leaning on using where we landed as the Guild HQ for this planet. I think this would make a good place for the Guild's planet HQ; nice and smooth landing area and plenty of room for building on the site."

Anya finished her first cup of coffee, got up and went to the machine for a second. The aroma of the freshly brewed coffee filled the shuttle, an aroma she loved. She had always needed that second jolt of coffee at the beginning of the mission and did not mind sacrificing her coffee on the last day to get it.

Sulligan got up from the table and walked over to the side portal across from him. He just gazed out over the planets surface for a few minutes. He then moved to the front of the shuttle to his command seat to begin the check-down procedure that was his responsibility at the start of each day. The checklist was long and would take him over thirty minutes. There were no short-cuts on the list, their safety while planet bound depended on it. They were entirely on their own and they could not afford for him to miss a single detail.

Anya walked over to the side portal facing the back of the shuttle and looked at the track of their touchdown on this First Landing. She had finished her second mug of coffee and still had time before Sulligan had finished his prep for the day. She thought of Gustof on his farm. He would have written down the exact minute of their touchdown on the planet for her to see when she got home. It had become a ritual of theirs. Through three missions now they were married and somehow he knew the moment of each landfall. She caught the reflection of her face in the portal; oval shaped, light brown eyes, dark hair and her smile that Gustof said kept him alive. She thought again of Gustof. How did he know when she landed?

Anya thought back to their first breakfast as a married couple. Her cooking breakfast, pancakes, and Gustof coming up from behind her and putting his arms around her. It had felt so warm and loving.

Finally she broke the silence and gave her first order of the day to Sulligan. "We head to the mountains we passed on our way down."

"Sulligan looked up from his readings and replied, surprised by her directions.

"Not the ruins," he questioned.

Anya walked over to the navigation/charting control screen that was placed behind her command chair. She could easily swivel her chair and view it when they were moving. For future missions on this planet a communication consol would be placed there. A third explorer would be added to the crew as well for that. Right now they had no need of communications; there was nobody to communicate with.

"I have a hunch, Sully. We will save the ruins for the end of the mission. Without the aerial surveillance we will need to cover as much ground as possible in the shuttle." She almost added, 'and those mountains are drawing me to them.'

Sulligan looked back at his commander as he started up the shuttles electric engine. The fully deployed solar sail was working and the capacitors showed a full charge. Sulligan saw she had a slight frown on her face.

"All ahead Captain, Mame," he half-laughed, "we're off to find the Wizard." Even that reference to her favorite classic video failed to gain a smile on her face. Sulligan knew she missed her husband.

The shuttle started moving across the flat plain that they had landed on, running parallel to their landing tracks. It gave them some orientation to where the mountains were hiding over the horizon from them.

"Off to see the Wizard," she hummed half-heartedly back at Sulligan.

~ ~ ~ ~ ~

Gustof sat in his kitchen, a half-drunk cup of coffee loosely held in his right hand. He didn't really care for it but he drank it when she was gone on mission. The taste and aroma made her seem closer. A half-eaten scone with apricot jam sat on a small plate on the table next to him. Both of Gustof's dogs sat outside the force-screen of the outside door. The force-screen was set to his and his wife's body frequencies so he need not bother shut it off unless there was company. That was rare when she was gone.

Canines had changed physically through bioengineering; they lived longer and healthier lives. Something that had not changed was that they still gave their unconditional love to their masters. 'Why could not people be that way?' he thought. He tried to understand his wife and the tremendous joy she got from her missions. However being apart for periods of six months at a time affected his daily life.. The Guild had discouraged their marriage because of that, relenting only when their rising star and Gustof refused to change their minds.

The thoughts kept creeping in; at times, he was powerless to stop them. Her and Sulligan, alone on that planet, what did they do together in their down time?

Gustof got up and walked out through the force-screen to play with his dogs. The days planting would wait for another day.

~ ~ ~ ~ ~

The mountain range was more distant than she thought from the flyover. With the flatness of the terrain and lack of visual perspective they checked their direction several times; they were right on course. The surface radar showed no irregularities to the horizon. The navigation/charting computer was doing its mapping automatically of everything within range. There was little for them to do right now as the shuttle chugged along at a little over fifteen mph.

"We should have started with the ruins," Sulligan said ruefully.

"Where and when we go is up to use alone, its time to take some pictures and enjoy the scenery," Anya responded, getting up from her command seat to stretch, the controls all set to automatic. An alarm would sound if the radar spotted any anomalies around them.

Sulligan started working the cameras while the Anya turned in her command seat to face the nav station behind her. The terrain was flat with few elevations more than a few dozen feet to the horizon. As Anya stared at the video screen there an anomaly appeared on the screen. Just to the starboard side of their dead ahead course was the reading that concerned her. (Perhaps being concerned was too strong a word). She definitely thought that it deserved watching. It was probably nothing. However, with her five missions behind her she had learned never to ignore anything out of the ordinary. No matter how insignificant it looked.

~ ~ ~ ~ ~

Anya remembered telling Gustof about the one time such a reading had gone ignored. It was in her second mission with her old commander who had trained her. He was in a rush to finish a mining assessment of a promising area on an especially rich planet. And he was out to make a name for himself at the same time, something to be remembered by. This was his last mission; the magic number 9. He had considered it a slight when he had had to wait the full six missions to be named a Senior Explorer. It was ironic, his mistake in part led her to being noticed in the reports and eventually named a Senior Explorer a year earlier than normal, the first to be named Senior Explorer after just four missions. And it ended his career with the Guild.

"We were always taught, it was ingrained in us, or least was supposed to be. These new worlds were dangerous, even if it was not a First Landing or sending explorers wouldn't be needed. If they were safe the Miner's Guild would be on the planet after the first mission, not us. Its why the Explorer's Guild spends time on a planet before handing it over to another Guild."

They were sitting on the porch of his home. Gustof was already an accomplished farmer; soils and plants seemed a part of him. He had met the Anya at the Explorers Guild HQ right after her return from her second mission and she was getting ready for her next. He was part of a delegation from the Agg Guild. And they were in love the moment they met. She called him her anchor.

"What happened?" he excitedly asked, wrapped up in the story of the world she had just explored.

"The anomaly on the radar looked small. Its ground radar but it does pick up slight irregularities sub-surface. It was a cavern, a large one, with just a thin brittle shell of surface area covering it. The ground started to cave in as the surface cracked under us. Only the rear wheels still had traction when I deployed the holding anchor. It shot back about 80 feet behind us and dragged quite a ways before it stopped us, the anchor barely 20 feet from the edge but holding strong. The Explorer was not even at his station when it happened. He was at the back table, not even belted in, writing in his log. We're supposed to do that at the end of each day, not while we're moving. Anyways, it shot back far enough to hold us and keep us from going over the edge. As I started retracted the anchors cable, pulling us back from the opening, more soil crackled underneath us and gave way and the shuttle started to fall. I was attached my seat harness and called back to my commander to do the same. We banged pretty hard but the anchor held. I am not even 21, on my second mission, and I had to make the decisions that kept us alive without even having the training to do so.

As I retracted the first anchor, I shot the second into a high arch even further behind us. It caught and held us until we reached firm ground. The Senior Explorer was pretty badly hurt. It ended the mission short.

"That cavern was immense. He should have been in his command seat and seen it."

"Do all shuttle have these anchors?" he asked her, his eyes wide open.

"No, these were special tools the Senior Explorer of the First Landing had recommended all shuttles carry on this planet. Ours was the first to have two of them. Within two more missions, they were standard on all shuttles. The one smart thing my Senior Explorer did was to have them installed. With his neglect of the nav station, one would not have been enough. The cavern was over a half a mile deep and over a mile across. Even a few seconds more..." She started to shake as she remembered the story.

"You could have died," Gustof said, a tear in his eye as he pulled her tight. It was this story that changed how he felt about her missions as he realized the danger she faced with each.

"Yes, we both could have died. I leaned an important lesson there though, something to carry forward on my missions. The importance of everything around us, no matter how trivial or small it may appear, on a planet"

To the Guild it taught her even more; the importance of her attention to detail and safety. That led to her first promotion to Explorer for her next mission. and her promotion to Senior Explorer after just five missions and a First Landing mission, with Sulligan now as her apprentice for a second time.

~ ~ ~ ~ ~

Anya called Sulligan over to her nav station from the camera station. "Just leave them on automatic; we have plenty of file space. I need you to watch something."

Sulligan got up quickly and stood behind where she was sitting at the nav station. He could hear some concern in her voice.

"Here, on the edge of the charting," she used her finger to point out the anomaly as she spoke. "It may be nothing. It could be significant. And it looks like we'll be crossing it."

She turned from the nav station and motioned for Sulligan to take her place at it. "I need for you to watch this and keep me informed of its position or any changes, no matter how small in the readings."

"Yes," was all Sulligan said as he took the place seat vacated by his Commander.

"I'll be in the command seat," Anya said, "its time to slow down and take over manual control. There is something there. I can feel it."

The shuttle slowed to a crawl as they approached the anomaly. She brought the shuttle to a stop at the edge of it, a wide shallow valley. This had been a river once, an important find for so early in their mission. Sulligan took a mineral reading with the spectroscope; nothing of significance on the surface of the dry river.

The banks of the dry river were shallow, worn down by the countless millennia since the planet had lost most of its atmosphere. Even a limited atmosphere leads to erosion. They sped across the wide dry riverbed, the Senior Explorer at the controls and climbed the bank on the other side. Her finger never strayed far from the anchor's release. She still remembered that time from before.

The Radar showed no further anomalies ahead.

~ ~ ~ ~ ~

Gustof was still unloading his truck from the trip to the co-op when he saw dust on the road into his farm. It only took him a second to recognize Stefen's car driving in. Gustof wasn't sure if he was happy or sad about the visit. He still had the supplies for the greenhouse to unload.

Stefen came to a stop next to Gustof's truck.

"You know they have robots for that," Stefen good-naturedly said as he got out of his car. "Here, let me lend you a hand."

Stefen reached into the back of the truck and grabbed a box, loading it onto the cart Gustof was loading. "You have a lot here."

"They are supplies that just came into the co-op for me from the Explorer's Guild. They're to help me in the greenhouse with the work I do for them."

They loaded the cart quickly from the truck with Stefen's help.

"You know, Gustof, most of the farms around here have help from the Agg Guild. If you need any extra help I'll be around for another week in the area. Not much else than paperwork to do right now. I could come over each day and give you a hand with the farm. I don't get to do much farm work these days. Its mostly just the Guild's paperwork."

Gustof hesitated. He appreciated his offer, the greenhouse alone was a lot of work at times, but this was a special project for the Explorer's Guild.

"I can still manage it for now," he said as he set the carts controls for the entrance to the greenhouse. "Anya helps me whenever she's earthbound."

"I can tell you miss her, don't you."

"Sometimes," Gustof answered, "But I'm with her and she's with me even when we are separated by the vast distances of space."

The two men followed behind the cart on foot the hundred yards or so to the greenhouse. Stefen couldn't believe how large it was when he got up close.

"This is all for your work, Gustof? I'm a little envious of you."

He was more than a little envious of Gustof's project. His own research for the Guild had been on better food choices to be introduced to the colony planets. He had thought the grant from the Explorer's Guild would be his. He tried to hide his jealousy of Gustof getting it instead of himself. He had counted on that grant and then nothing. And then, at the last moment, Gustof had stepped in with his soy bean improvements and the Explorer's Guild had jumped at the idea.

"This place is really something," Stefen said, in true admiration of what Gustof had accomplished. "Can I give you a hand at carrying all of this in?"

"Sure, we'll just stack them inside the outer door."

"Outer door? What is this, top secret?"

"Sort of," Gustof quickly said as they each carried a box into the greenhouse's entry foyer and put the boxes on a shelf.

"Can I see inside, or is that off-limits," Stefen asked as they finished stacking the boxes.

Gustof was happy to show the greenhouse to somebody from the Agg Guild. He would appreciate it more than the visitors from the

Explorer's Guild. Gustof closed the outer door and then opened the inner door. Force screens kept anything from outside getting in. The inside of the greenhouse was as big as a rugby field. Rows after rows of containers with their sow bean plants, from those just planted to ones over six feet tall."

"Is this what you won your grant with?" Stefen asked, both amazed and jealous of Gustof's work.

'Yes," Gustof answered, wondering where Stefen had found out about the grant. "I've put it to great use for the Explorer's Guild. They're really happy with what I've already accomplished here and have [promised me more research money." Gustof wished he hadn't said that the moment it came out of his mouth.

"It doesn't hurt to have Anya in your corner," Stefen said, almost snidely, as he walked to a long container of soil, his hands in his pockets.

Gustof just stopped what he was doing and looked at Stefen.

"I received the grant before I met her," was his stiff response. "Just why are you here, Stefen."

"No offence meant, old buddy," Stefen said, smiling at Gustof. "I heard about the grant through the Agg Guild and just wanted to see an old buddy from school and congratulate him. You are almost part of the Explorer's Guild aren't you?"

Stefen took his hands out of his pockets and ran them through the soil. "How do you get such rich soil. Other farms I've visited aren't half this good," Stefen said with admiration.

"I make my own mulch and compost. It's enough for my greenhouse. I still have to use Agg Guild fertilizer on the rest of the farm."

The two of them walked the length of the greenhouse and back. Several times on the walk Stefen ran his hands through the rich soil.

As they left the greenhouse and walked back to Stefen's car, Stefen asked one more time if Gustof needed any help.

"I'm good for now. It was great seeing you after all these years. Stay in touch."

"You too. And I'm sorry for that remark about Anya and the Explorer's Guild."

"That's OK," Gustof said. "I guess in some ways I'm as much apart of the Explorer's Guild as the Agg Guild."

As Stefen got into his car to leave he called out to Gustof, "I'll mention the great work you are doing here."

"Thanks," Gustof called back as he walked to his combine. There was still work to do on the farm. He thought of Anya and her Guild. "I guess I really am part of that now."

~ ~ ~ ~ ~

The explorers finally stopped the shuttle for the night, the mountains sitting in the distance, still a long ways off.

Sulligan, after finishing up his nightly shuttle shutdown operations, following the guidelines of the Guild, walked to the back of the shuttle and folded out the table from the wall.

"Cribbage?" Sulligan asked Anya who was stretching as she got up from her command seat.

"How about a video?" Anya answered Sulligan in the back of the shuttle. She took a last look out the front windows of the shuttle. With little atmosphere the stars shown brilliantly as the sun went down over the horizon.

Sulligan enthusiastically responded to the idea. "A classic film noir? I'll make the popcorn." This was a commonality they had; they both enjoyed watching the videos from the first century of movie making.

They sat on the cushioned bench that folded out of the wall across from the fold-down table. The video screen was on the wall now above the table where it folded out. Anya had had the large panel video screen installed for them on this shuttle before the trip, another perk of being the youngest Senior Explorer, ever. The bag of popcorn sat on the table in front of them for them both to enjoy.

Some explorers read, some wrote, some enjoyed their music, art or even just meditation on the long exploration voyages. For Anya and Sulligan it was cribbage and old classic movies. They had installed over one thousand hours of videos to choose from for the trip and they never tired of them.

Chapter 4

The next morning they redeployed the solar sail and began the long journey ahead of them to the mountains, now clearly visible in the distance. As they traveled across the dry plain they continued to discover more anomalies in the ground. All were dry riverbeds. This planet must have been covered in water in its distant past. Several of the dried up riverbeds they crossed were almost a mile across.

They reached the base of the mountains in the short twilight of nightfall. In the changing shadows of the fast setting sun, the mountain range looked like nothing but precipices and cliffs.

"Any good readings from the radar," Anya asked Sulligan who was sitting in front of the navigation screen. She was sitting in her command chair of the shuttle, looking ahead at the grays of the landscape with its rapidly shifting shadows from the planets sun behind them. Radar had come a long ways over the centuries and it was showing detailed images of what lay before them. Anya kept working on her share of the nighttime shutdown procedures while she waited for Sulligan's reply. She looked outside at the changing browns and grays of the landscape.

"Nothing appears on the screen that we hadn't seen earlier. It does not look to be as rugged as it looks out the portal. It's funny how the shadows can play tricks on the mind. With daylight, it looks like we will have several promising paths into the mountains to check out. Do you have anything in mind that we will be looking for?" Sulligan knew that it would be up to future missions to search for the mineral wealth that was one of the goals of advanced missions once the Explorers were done.

Rare mineral wealth of the explored planets of the Guild funded further explorations and First Landings. The need for these minerals on Earth and its colonies was great. The Earth had given up the last of its easily attained mineral wealth hundred of years earlier in a frenzied last dig by the worlds powerful. Huge stretches of world's oceans were destroyed in the feeding frenzy for what remained of the rare minerals that were needed for everyday life. And the planet had almost died.

As the mineral wealth ran out, the world plunged into a depression that took almost a hundred years to recover. Wealth became so consolidated in the few that their share of that wealth stagnated and then began to shrink rapidly as people came to realize that they actually had no need for those few and their reminders of past greed. Governments fell, no longer able to supply the people with what hope they needed.

A new market system, a true sharing free market economy arose. No longer were the central states dictating every move of business as the world had become smaller. Co-ops, family business and individual initiative overtook the old order. It took the old infrastructure that the world could not longer support and rebuilt the world, one small step at a time. In time this new order simply ignored the old central states and the *elites* who supported them. Finally, the old order collapsed in the face of the worlds changing needs.

Individual needs interacted with societies and new avenues of growth emerged as solutions were found to problems that arose. New initiatives brokered new thoughts and from this, co-ops merged to found the origins of the Explorer's Guild as the people of Earth began once more to look to the heavens.

The technology was there to reach the closest stars. Even an attempt at colonization was tried fifty years before the founding of the Guild. It was lost, a failure, with no communication from it for years. When found, only the last skeletal remains of the expedition were recovered. There were no survivors and it became known to the Explorer's Guild as the Lost Roanoke Expedition; the lessons learned from it passed on to future colonies.

The Explorer's Guild formed from three co-ops, led by an engineering co-op. They found and took existing technology and incorporated that which had been used by the failed colonial attempt. From past successes and failures of exploration on earth they began to build a model that would work going forward. Their goal was not to repeat the mistakes of history but to be willing to learn from them.

What remained of the old wealth sneered at their ideas; they were no longer relevant. Enough of the shared market economy got on board with the project to allow a First Landing attempt to be launched.

Before selecting the planet destined to become the first First Landing, the Guild commissioned the world's astronomers and their own Guild to search for those stars whose planets might contain the greatest amount of mineral wealth. They did not know if they would find life. They almost hoped they wouldn't. However, perhaps a beneficial trade deal could be worked out. And, if not trade with another world at least an empty planet would provide the mineral wealth Earth so badly needed.

A planet was chosen, after a year of running the search algorithms. The three-person mission was prepared and trained: another year and a half of expenses draining the coffers of the Guild. They held another round of crowd-funding, this time many of the world's people contributing just a little. But it was enough, barely, to at least ensure the endeavor would continue through the explorers return.

Bonanza. The First Landing. An uninhabited planet, it had just enough atmosphere and water to allow the Minor's Guild, the third Guild to join the Explorer's Guild, to work. There were enough rare minerals on the surface to ensure that the Guild would never be in need of funding again; a wealth to be shared by all of its millions of crowd-share investors.

A new economic golden age appeared on earth and the Explorer's Guild led the way. Old wealth and old idea's fell to the back roads of the past. A new vibrancy, a path to the stars, took hold on the Earth. And nobody wanted to be left behind.

With this new economic Golden Age the Explorer's Guild broke once more into its component parts. Each Guild was defined and given its task in the explorations to come.

The Explorer's Guild would lead the way with its First landings and initial exploration of the planets they found.

Once done the Miner's Guild would take over, bringing the mineral wealth of the universe back to the Earth's expanding economic empire.

The Agriculture Guild was given the job of developing the food needed for deep space exploration and the first colonies. The lessons of the Roanoke Expedition were learned and developed here.

The Engineering Guild would become responsible for the construction of the first space modules and systems for the Explorer's Guild to continue its explorations of the universe and the first planetary living modules for the Miner's Guild.

There were the occasional cries of the rape of other worlds. The past had almost destroyed the Earth with humanity right along. But these were empty worlds they mined, unsuitable for colonization. First Landings were still trying to find other than primitive life.

They did find the remains of what must have at one time been an advanced culture on one of the barren worlds. From these findings a new Guild arose in the Guild's Hierarchy. The archeologist Guild, whose job it was to explore that past civilization and learn something from it.

Two worlds were found, within a year of each other, rich, hospitable, with primitive life found. Here the first rules of colonization were developed. No mining was allowed on these worlds or any world found containing life. There was no need. The richness of the universe was all around them in its dead or dying worlds and it seemed it was destined to belong solely to the Earth.

Within a year a third hospitable world was found and people began to rush to these new worlds, proving grounds for each person's idea of what utopia was. A new Guild was formed, the New Colony Guild. They would simply publish a crowd-funding notice for a new world and wait for the people to line up for the next trip.

There might be conflicts in the future but with the Explorer's Guild's over-riding reach and emphasis on human rights and dignity, these conflicts were minimal. There was more than enough room for all beliefs.

One conflict, short-lived, was over the fishing rights of a large fresh water sea on the First Colony. The Guild came down hard on both sides. Without the assets of the Guilds neither side could hope to survive long enough to establish themselves. There hadn't been a conflict of note since.

~ ~ ~ ~ ~

It was two weeks since Stefen's visit to the farm and Gustof hadn't been to the co-op since that time. He had been working hard installing new equipment into the greenhouse and planting a sector of the new seed the Explorer's Guild had sent him to work with.

Gustof loved working in the greenhouse; the feel of the rich soil in his hands. Everything done in the greenhouse Gustof did by hand. Half of the auto equipment the Guild had sent him still remained in its crates.

The new work had been a bit overwhelming for him. Gustof had to admit he was feeling a little lethargic. Nothing surprising to him, he had been working 14 hour days with Anya gone. It was definitely time for a break.

Gustof called his two dogs to him after breakfast. He had to admit to himself he hadn't been eating well lately. Just the hard work and fatigue he thought. He was still wearing the same clothes he had worked and slept in the last few days. He'd shower and change, he thought to himself, when he got back from the co-op. He got into the truck, his dogs jumping right into the front of the truck with him.

The dogs loved the trip to the co-op. They could run around and greet everybody there.

Gustof parked in front of the co-op and let his dogs out of the truck. The dogs immediately ran over to an area set aside for the co-op member's dogs, a self-cleaning grassy area, and joined the other dogs already there in play.

Gustof walked through the air curtain door of the co-op and the store clerk, Amanda, immediately saw Gustof half-stumble into the store. Amanda was a little surprised at how he looked. Gustof was always cleaned up when he came to the co-op, Anya made sure of that. He looked tired and a little disheveled.

'Overwork, lack of sleep and he misses Anya' Amanda thought.

Amanda called over to Gustof, "No packages for you today." She expected some sort of response from Gustof. He always said hello when he came into the store, greeting everybody there. This time nothing, not even a smile.

Gustof just walked around the store, haphazardly picking up groceries for the dogs and himself. Amanda kept watching him. He picked up a case of soda and put it into the cart.

'He doesn't drink soda,' Amanda thought to herself. She started walking over to Gustof as he loaded his cart. Gustof just loaded his cart seemingly randomly; he was putting things into his cart he just didn't buy. 'That's wrong,' she thought.

Gustof walked over to the coffee stand at the back of the store and poured himself a cup. 'Coffee was Anya's drink when she came in, not Gustof's. He would go over to the pub next door and have an ale with his friends when he was done shopping; coffee, never. Now she was getting a little concerned about Gustof.

Amanda joined Gustof at the coffee counter.

"Gustof. I haven't seen you in a few weeks."

"Just busy," he lackadaisically answered, barely looking at her. "Just a lot of work."

Amanda tried a joke. Gustof always laughed at her jokes, funny or not; nothing

"So how is the rocket-woman?" That was her nickname for Anya and Gustof always laughed and smiled at it. Again nothing, not even a smile.

Amanda followed Gustof to the checkout are and then helped him load his truck. She didn't question what he bought; maybe it was for friends he had coming over. Amanda tried to coax some sort of response out of him as he called his dogs and got into the truck. He didn't even bother going to the pub next store or say hello to his friends standing outside. He just climbed into his truck and drove off.

Amanda watched him drive away. Gustof could be quiet when Anya was away, but this wasn't Gustof at all. She began to worry about her friend. 'Maybe he just misses Anya.' However, she would go to the pub after work and tell their friends about how he was acting. Something just wasn't right with Gustof.

~ ~ ~ ~ ~

"Do you want to deploy the jet-drone tomorrow," Sulligan asked Anya as he worked his checklist for shutting down the shuttle for the night. The Solar Sail had just finished retracting and he was checking the capacitors load for the evening. They had a small amount of diesel fuel as an emergency energy supply. But it was just that, a very small emergency supply. The capacitors showed a full load. They would be fine with whatever this world brought them overnight. They still had no idea of what the nighttime temps would be, but with the limited atmosphere it would be cold, very cold.

"I think we will put off using the jet-drone. Hindsight being what it is we should have brought a second, something to pass onto to future missions."

"They thought we had an atmosphere," replied Sulligan, looking up from his checklist.

"The problem with earth bound readings and why First Landings are so important. How are the readings, Sulligan?"

"Everything looks strong and secure. I deployed our anchors for and aft in case of high winds."

"Then lets finish the shutdown," the Senior Explorer ordered. "Then we will go over together the preliminary info on the radars and choose our course for starting out tomorrow." She continued looking at the fading images of the mountains as darkness overtook them. The shadows receded quickly now from the setting sun. With the limited atmosphere this planets twilight and early morning pre-light would be short lived.

"All done, Captain, Mame," Sulligan crisply offered to his commander, trying to elicit a smile from the sadness he saw on her face from the reflection of the forward portal. He knew she was thinking of Gustof as she looked out. She briefly smiled as she got up from her command chair and moved to the rear of the shuttle.

Sulligan finished his work, got up from his command seat and walked to the back table, "Cribbage?"

"How about a video'" the Senior Explorer answered back as she got up from her command seat and moved to the back as well.

"A classic noir? I'll get the popcorn," he enthusiastically responded to her. The popcorn is what Sulligan had used his bonus food allotment for, not much, but enough for them when they watched the videos. This was a commonality they held. They both enjoyed watching the videos from the first century of movie making.

They sat on the cushioned bench, the bag of popcorn between them, having turned it to face a screen in one of the interior wall panels. She had installed this large screen before the trip, another prerogative of being a Senior Explorer.

Some explorers wrote, some read, some enjoyed music, art, or even just meditation on the long journeys. For the Senior Explorer and Sulligan it was cribbage and old classic videos. They tired of neither.

~ ~ ~ ~ ~

Gustof was sitting back in his reading chair, his dogs at his feet. The reader he held was about the latest techniques for making his Soy plants more resistant to insects, the bane of farmers' from the beginning of time. Both his dogs were asleep near his feet. It was late but he had not been able to sleep. That was becoming more difficult when she was away on mission. He looked over at the 3D picture of her on the lamp stand. Every time she returned from space she looked more beautiful he thought. Was that the effect of space or just his longings for her? Did Sulligan notice how beautiful she was? Gustof tried to push that thought from his mind. The last few weeks that had become harder to do. This time he could not as a tear came to his eye with a light sob. One of his dogs looked up at him as if to say, 'Are you alright, master.' Sleep finally came to him in the chair, but it was a fitful sleep.

It was two nights before Amanda was able to go to the co-ops pub. Ordering and follow-up for the store had kept her late there. Everything was supposed to be automatic, but she found if she didn't double check the orders, mistakes were made. When she finally made it there she didn't forget about Gustof's fitful state when he was at the store. As she entered she saw Michael, Gustaf's friend from university and several other of their friends sitting at a table on the far side of the pub. She smiled their way as she walked to the bar to get an ale. They waved her over and she walked over to the table, ale in hand, and joined them.

"How are you doing, Amanda?" Michael asked as she grabbed a chair and sat down at the table.

"I'm doing OK. Have any of you seen Gustof lately?" she asked the table.

"No we haven't, but a big rugby match is coming up. Gustof's always up for those."

"What's up?" Philip asked. He had heard the concern in Amanda's voice when she asked about Gustof.

"He was in the store the other day and he didn't seem right."

"It was probably just him missing Anya," Michael said. "Who know how he is when she is away on a mission."

"That's what I thought at first, he just misses her. But there was more, I can feel it. What he bought that day just wasn't Gustof."

"A doppelganger?" Mark laughed.

"No," Amanda frowned as she spoke. "I think something is wrong. I'm concerned."

"I'll tell you what Amanda. I have the day off tomorrow. I'll swing by his place and see how he is," Phillip answered.

"I'll go too," Mark said.

"Me too," Michael added. "I'll use the excuse of inviting him on the road trip to the Big match."

"Just let me know," Amanda almost pleaded. "I think that he needs our help."

Chapter 5

It was during the first nightfall on the planet and the two explorers were awakened by the shuttle's alarms. The satellite had picked up on its long range sensors a mass heading into the planets orbit; Cosmic matter, a rock or even a dust cloud. It was still too distant to classify fully. Not that they could do much whatever it was and from its distance and speed they had at least a few weeks of exploration before they had to do anything about it. When the approaching objects real trajectory was known, then a decision would have to be made; to end the mission early or not. The satellite had no screens or defenses and if their long range craft was damaged they would be unable to return home.

The next morning began abruptly, like the evening had ended the night before. The landscape moved from darkness to the grays of the early shadows to the browns of this planets bleak surface.

Bleak to an Earthlander, to the Senior Explorer and her apprentice, Sulligan, this landscape was the most beautiful that they had ever seen. The low hills in front of them led to a high elevation of the ranges peaks. There appeared to be gaps in the peaks, passes that would enable them to see what lay on the other side of this range.

A quick mug of coffee, reconstituted eggs and then their excitement threatened to overtake them. The danger of First Landing Euphoria is what the Guild called it. They had been warned in training to expect it. But this was their third mission together they reasoned. The two had been confident that they could avoid it. In this they were proven wrong in the morning's early light.

Sulligan had his checklist to start the day, beginning with the deployment of the Solar Sail. This was his responsibility alone, the deployment at the start of each day and its retraction at night for protection, would have a lot to say how successful their mission would be. This was their power source and, if sufficiently damaged, it would mean having to call the mission short.

Sulligan had his tasks, ingrained into the life of the apprentice, to see him through the early affects of the Euphoria. For the Senior Explorer there were no such ingrained tasks. Hers was one; explore the new world to prepare the Guild for future missions there. She looked out the front of the command seat and she could not escape the wonder of what she saw, what the first person from Earth on this planet saw. She knew it would lead to a waste of their precious amount of air, but she had to stand on the planet, to feel its soil in her hand.

"Sully, we are going out," she told her friend as she got up from the command seat.

Sulligan had just started his checklist when she said this. Already setting back into routine, and with that the effects of the Euphoria leaving him, he asked her when.

"Now, Sully, while the dawn is still fresh."

"I'll check the soil and atmosphere readings next then. We should have the safety results in an hour or so."

The Euphoria still held his commander. "Now, Sully, I'll go get our breathing apparatus and we can go."

Sulligan looked up from his now almost completed checklist and saw the ecstatic look on her face. "I will be ready in just a minute. You go get the masks from storage for us to use while I finish my checklist."

She hurried to the back of the shuttle to its supply closet to retrieve the masks.

Several previous missions had been lost at this point and it was as much to prevent the effects of the Euphoria that the checklist and its importance had been developed. It assured that at least one member of the crew would be in command of their reason before any serious damage was done.

With the Senior Explorer busy in the supply closet, digging past everything it seemed to find the masks (intentionally put in the very back for the reason of the Euphoria) Sulligan reached down beneath his station and locked the shuttle doors with his thumb on the kill-switch. The commander had a similar kill-switch at her consul. Now, only he could open the shuttles doors. These switches were a necessary precaution against Euphoria or Space Sickness. There had been some on-board conflicts and shortened missions with the kill-switches, but no more crews had been lost to this aspect of First Landing.

Sulligan hoped that there would be no issues with his Senior Explorer over his lockdown of the shuttle. If he could delay her long enough he knew the Euphoria would wear off.

Sulligan walked to the small galley and set the coffee maker to brewing a mug. The aroma of the fresh coffee started to refill the shuttle, for a time overpowering the air conditioner of the small vessel. The Senior Explorer came forward to the galley from the supply cabinet with a breathing devise in each hand.

"Sully," she said, seemingly surprised at the fresh brewed coffee, "a second mug for you."

"No, it's for you. I thought that you could use the second cup, the extra caffeine today. I took it from my rations for you. A gift before we set foot on this planets surface together."

"Sully, how thoughtful," she said, not thinking about their limited supplies. "You want to be first on the planet, don't you," she frowned.

"Not at all," he said as he handed her the mug. She took it in both hands and felt the warmth in her hands. She sat down in her euphoric state to enjoy the complexities of the coffee. Sulligan watched her become calm again as she savored her beverage. Sulligan's ruse had worked.

~ ~ ~ ~ ~

Gustof felt a cold chill come across his body. He shut down the tractor and just sat there for long while. She had had a close call. A very close call. He wondered again why did she have to keep putting herself in danger when they had each other now? He had talked to her before about his fears. 'I have to let this go, I know that its part of our life. I accepted that when I married her.' He went back to work on the tractor preparing the field.. It was all he could do.

~ ~ ~ ~ ~

The Senior Explorer was sitting in a seat against the back wall of the shuttle's living quarters. The mug of coffee was held mid-air, the two breathing devices on the table alongside her. She sat that way for a long time, just looking straight ahead. Sulligan had gone back to work at the nav station to review his plots for the start of the days journey. With this planet, they had about eleven hours of sunlight each day. As he worked he kept his eye on her.

Finally, she looked up and set down the mug of coffee on the table. She spoke.

"Euphoria," she said quietly to Sulligan. He just nodded his head.

She picked up the breathing equipment.

"These?"

"You wanted to pick up the planets soil and run it through your fingers."

"I wanted to do what? I do not remember a thing. You did the lock-down?" she asked.

Sulligan nodded yes at the question.

"Nice job, Sulligan. I'll put these away," she said as she picked up the breathing apparatus. "Nice job, Sully," she said quietly under her breath as she walked to the back storage closet of the shuttle to put the apparatus away. "Nice job."

~ ~ ~ ~ ~

Philip, Michael and Mark were sitting on Mark's porch, discussing what Amanda had said about Gustof the night before. They all realized how worried she seemed about him.

"You ready to head over," Michael asked.

"Yeah, let's go, we can take my truck," Philip said, getting up from his chair.

"It's probably nothing," Mark added.

~ ~ ~ ~ ~

Anya was sitting in her command chair, every control on manual. The shuttle was barely moving forward in a crawl. They had earlier entered a promising pass through the mountain after twice having to change course do to obstacles. Half of the day was now gone. Sulligan sat at the nav station behind her. Anomalies were appearing on the screen again, a lot of them.

Up to now this new path had seemed a good one. Anya got the feeling she was following a frequently traveled path of this long dead planet. She looked out the forward windows of the shuttle. The land was unnaturally flat to either side of the shuttles path and at time sheer cliff walls came right down to the valley floor. Natural or cut, it was hard to tell after a millennia of erosion. They kept to the center of the valley; debris from the cliffs lay along the walls of the valley on either side.

The radar anomalies continued all around them. She could see nothing. The radar said something was there.

"Stop!" Anya heard Sulligan shout out at her. She brought the shuttle to a quick halt.

"Something is out there," Sulligan reported. "Come take a look at the screen."

She turned from her command seat and walked to the station to see what Sulligan was alarmed about.

There it was. On the radar, it was only about a half a mile away, something large and solid. She looked out the side portal in the direction the radar said it stood. She should be able to see whatever it was. There was nothing, nothing at all that was visible.

'What is out there?' she thought. 'It has to be something, the radar sees it.'

"Sully, get the jet-drone ready for launch, half of the fuel. Right now I wish I had brought a second one. We have to know what is out there. I will watch the nav station while you deploy it. Launch it 10 degrees to port and we should get a pretty good idea of what is out there."

"I will have to retract the solar sail for launch and recovery,' he said back to her, starting the launch procedure for the drone.

"Are we fully charged right now?"

"Batteries are over 99% storage right now," Sulligan answered.

"Launch the drone when you are ready, then redeploy the sail. We will retract it again when we recover the drone. I will watch as the results come in from here. You take the command seat for now. I'll tell you which way to move the shuttle and when."

The jet-drone was a little over ten feet long. It would launch from the shuttle on a catapult that also acted as its recovery arm. A single small jet powered it once it was clear of the shuttle, its wings extending outward. Made of carbon fiber and advanced metals, it was fairly light, and once its mission was completed it was designed to glide to a stop near the shuttle where the catapult/arm would collect it for its next use.

The wings extended as the drone was launched. Almost immediately, the jet kicked in and it shot skyward, taking a broad sweep to the right, following the preset course that Sulligan had programmed into it. Just as quickly the results of the drone's cameras, sensors and imaging radar were received back at the shuttle. What had been just anomalies on the shuttles charts was now filled in with detail.

All around them, underground, there was something sizable and solid. The cliff face to the left of the shuttle, half-covered with debris, now showed itself not to be a natural formation at all. Whatever it was, they were smack in the middle something left behind by whatever civilization had lived on this planet eons before.

It was nearing nightfall, too late to begin any significant exploration.

"Recall the drone, Sulligan. It looks like tomorrow we will get a chance to walk on the surface after all."

~ ~ ~ ~ ~

Gustof hadn't been to the pub and seen his friends in over three weeks. He was a regular there before he met Anya and even then he would frequently go there with her. When Anya was gone on mission it was almost like a second home for him, keeping his thoughts occupied with his friends; playing darts and discussing rugby.

Somehow, over the last few weeks, really since he had last seen Stefen, her mission seemed different this time. He couldn't shake it and wanted to be alone. Gustof felt trapped and he couldn't break out; his circle of life, his farm, his dogs and without Anya at his side was getting smaller. He felt it.

Gustof knew she wanted to be with him. In his heart he knew that they were destined to be as one. It was in his mind the many crazy images formed; crazy ones about her and Sulligan. He knew the thoughts were nonsense, but they kept coming back. He had to put his mind at rest; somehow. He tried to push the thoughts from his mind.

It was around lunch time when Gustof's friends from the pub pulled up to the house in Phillip's truck. Gustof was sitting on his porch with his dogs. The two dogs rushed down from the porch when the doors to the truck opened up and his friends spilled out. Gustof remained seated and barely looked at them.

Gustof looked even worse to them than Amanda described. He hadn't combed his hair and his beard, always short and well-trimmed, was a disheveled mess. His dirty clothes fell loosely over Gustof's gaunt body as he stood to greet his friends as they came up the steps to the porch. There were dark shadows under his eyes. And he stunk!

"We're not coming inside until you clean yourself up," Michael flat-out stated as he stood on the porch. "How long since you showered?"

"I... But... Not sure..." Gustof stammered.

Philip and Mark each grabbed an arm to take Gustof inside.

"And some clean clothes," Mark said.

"I don't know," Gustof half-resisted.

"Get in your shower before we throw you in ourselves," Phillip ordered.

Finally, Gustof demurred and climbed into the hot shower Phillip had turned on. It felt good.

The three friends tried to find a place to sit down while Gustof cleaned himself up. The place was such a mess they couldn't find one. Dirty clothes and garbage were all over. Finally, they just looked at each other, walked back out to the porch and sat down there.

Gustof finally joined them on the porch, wearing the same dirty clothes he had on when them arrived.

"Where are your clean clothes, Gustof?" Michael asked when Gustof came out. "You can't where those out here."

"I think that there are some in the closet," Gustof mumbled back. He just wanted to be left alone.

It took Michael a few minutes to find something half-way clean for Gustof to put on.

"Change into these Gustof," Michael smiles as he ordered Gustof to change and handed him the clothes. Something was definitely wrong with his friend. "We'll wait on the porch for you."

As Gustof slowly changed into the clothing that Michael had handed him he thought, 'What's the use.'

Michael watched Gustof change on the porch, he hadn't bother to go inside to change, and he was shocked when he saw the state of Gustof's body; ribs were showing and little muscle tone was left.

"When was the last time you ate?" Michael asked his long-time friend. Gustof was as big as any of them or least should have been. He had played full-back on the universities rugby team. And now…

As Gustof hesitated finishing getting dressed Mark stood up and walked over to him. "Let's go G, the gangs waiting for you at the pub. Chef's got a meat pie with your name on it. And Jack is bringing some of his special ale he brews for you to try."

Gustof tried to smile but his heart just wasn't in it. He was thinking of Anya, not with him, but in space with Sulligan.

Gustof spent the next four hours at the pub. His friends tried to encourage him to talk, but he stayed mostly quiet. He managed to finish the promised meat pie and chips; he was famished. And after the forth of Jack's special ale he wasn't feeling as much pain. However he still felt lost and lonely.

As they dropped him off back at his house Michael walked him back inside. He feed the dogs and looked around the mess one more time.

"Gustof, next week is the big rugby match at The Downs. You're coming with us."

Gustof tried to argue his way out of it. "My dogs, my farm, I can't go away for that many days."

"Jack's wife can take care of your dogs, It's her idea. Gives her a break from Jack."

"I can't leave the farm," Gustof pleaded.

"Your equipment can run itself. You're coming."

"What if there is news of Anya?" was Gustof's final attempt to get out of the road-trip.

"They'd reach you on your phone just as easily on the trip as here at your farm. It's just three days G. And you're coming!"

After Michael left he was alone again. Anya wasn't there with him like he needed. Tears came to his eyes before sleep found him on the bed, his two dogs curled up alongside him.

~ ~ ~ ~ ~

It was hot in the full sunlight of the early morning when they left the shuttle the next day. The night had proven uneventful and after watching a video of one of the *Thin Man* movies they both got a restful sleep. No further warnings from the satellite of the still approaching object in space came in.

When they stepped onto the surface of the planet the ground was fairly solid under their feet. What had shown up as anomalies on the nav screen of the shuttle they could now clearly see. Weathered and corroded bits of metal left from what had been built here long ago.

They both wore lightweight breathing devises for the thin atmosphere of the planet. Sulligan tried breathing on his own, but with little oxygen in the thin atmosphere, he quickly switched back to the breathing apparatus. While some oxygen remained, there wasn't enough to support them for even a short time. However, and this was important, the oxygen concentrators of the shuttle would be able to use the atmosphere to restore any oxygen they lost.

The two of them stood side by side and slowly turned three hundred and sixty degrees as they marveled at what they could now see so clearly around them; bits of metal, shinning through the corrosion in the sunlight. Never before had such a complete complex from the past been discovered on any planet; always it had been just bits and pieces of what had come before. Here was an ancient city, much of its former glory still visible, of a long lost past alien civilization.

~ ~ ~ ~ ~

Gustof was sitting on his porch watching the sunset as he so often did these days. A productive day on the tractor and he was back on track with his planting. The two dogs were in the distance chasing a ground squirrel they never caught. He was wearing clean clothes. He had done a load of laundry after his friend's intervention. However, he hadn't touched his house or kitchen and they were still a mess. What was the point of that? He had a book in his hands, real paper, not a video like so many read now. It was a book, a mystery novel, which Anya had given him. It gave him a connection to the past and to the firm ground that was at his feet. He remembered when she gave him the book. How pretty she looked as she walked up to him on the porch after she got out of her car. She had bent over him in his chair, giving him a wonderful kiss, the book held behind her back, wrapped in a bright paper covered in flowers.

He had asked her, "What did I do to deserve that kiss?"

She answered him, "Nothing, just being who you are."

He briefly looked up to the stars, her star. He could feel her discovery in his soul, something tremendous he knew. It made him proud and sad at the same time. His wife, the Senior Explorer, he knew had made a major find. But she did it alongside another. The thoughts of her and Sulligan together six months at a time, horrible thoughts of them together, just would not leave his mind anymore. He tired, he knew they weren't true. But they just wouldn't leave.

He thought of her words to him when she left on this mission, arms around each other, not wanting to let go.

"You are my anchor, Gustof, my love." The thought of her words briefly calmed his agitated mind. These respites from his darker thoughts were becoming fewer and of shorter duration. He missed her so much it hurt. And she was alone with Sulligan.

~ ~ ~ ~ ~

It would take a separate mission from the archeologist Guild, and probably a permanent station here, to fully explore the city that they had found. Already Sulligan was working to collect specimens and to catalogue their findings. He had already given thought to joining that Guild when his time with the Explorer's Guild were over. Many used the Explorer's Guild as a stepping stone to further their careers with other Guilds. The thought of living on and exploring alien worlds and their past civilizations thrilled him.

For the Senior Explorer, Anya, although she was also thrilled by their find, it was still just a First Landing mapping expedition, first and foremost. Others would follow her work and suggestions in detail. She knew of Sulligan's dreams; he had often mentioned them to her.

Once they returned she would work to help him achieve his dream. Maybe on this world, the Guild could use explorers of Sulligan's ability to lead the work here. It wasn't unusual for a member of the Explorer's Guild to jump right into a senior position with another Guild. Anya was impressed with how well he had dealt with the Euphoria. She would have to give him some tests on this mission, see how close he was to ready. She had not been held back when she had proven herself a year early. She did not think Sulligan should be held back as well if he was ready. And that was still a big if. She began to think of which Guild she would join once her time with the Explorer's Guild was through, something Earthbound, for Gustof.

They stopped their local exploration of the site at the planet's noon. The heat was getting oppressive. Sulligan had collected over ten pounds of samples. The samples weight would take the place of the weight of the items they used up on the trip. However, she could already tell that they would have to jettison some of their nonessential materials for the trip home to make room for all of the samples.

Anya watched Sulligan as a proud parent watches their child as he grew more excited with each find.

"After a quick meal, we'll take the shuttle to the opposite side of this find, several miles from here," Anya informed Sulligan as they boarded the shuttle, "further up the pass. That is where we will stop for the night. That will give you a chance to finish cataloguing your finds tonight. Tomorrow we will spend the morning exploring that side of this city, if that's what we have found, before we move on over the mountains."

She did not have to look at Sulligan's face; she could almost feel his smile as she said this. His eye's lit up like a child's when they discover new things around them.

'Yes,' she thought to herself, 'the Archeologist Guild is where he belongs. I will make sure that happens for him.' There were perks that came with attaining the rank of Senior Explorer.

Sulligan was up early the next morning. He had his checklist done, the solar sail deployed, and even their breakfast ready by the time the Senior Explorer had finished refreshing herself. His excitement to start the day was palpable. From the radar readings alone it appeared this area was even richer in relics than the area they had been in the day before. From a side portal Sulligan saw a sheet of some material half-buried in the ground. Even from the shuttle, it appeared to have some sort of glyphs or writing on it. It was too big to take with them but Sulligan could take images of the glyphs and bring them back with them. Now it was just the sheer joy of discovery, not the Euphoria of before.

"You can have all day here, Sulligan," she told her friend who was acting like an expectant father. "But tomorrow we start early to get over the pass by nightfall."

Sulligan began the day by imaging what he found on the large sheet of material he had seen. It extended deep into the ground the radar told him. How deep he could not tell. As Sulligan worked on the metal sheet, collecting his data, Anya began a long circular walk around the site. She was not thinking of Sulligan or the discovery. Her thoughts were of her husband, her anchor, Gustof, so far away on planet Earth. There were times she wished it was he with her. And this was one of those times.

As Anya walked somewhat absent-mindedly around their discovery, she tripped over something protruding from the ground, not enough to fall, but enough for her to take notice of what had tripped her. This was not a rock or rise in the ground she had caught her foot on, it was a solid metal loop, no more than an inch high above the dirt. They could have walked by it a dozen times and never seen it in the weathered ground it blended in so well.

'Thank-you, Gustof,' she said aloud as she looked up into the stars.

When she finally got Sulligan's attention and called him over he wanted to open up whatever they had found immediately.

"That is not for us, Sulligan. That is for the future, when the archeologist set up here. We have a lot to explore on this planet's over 200 million square miles to get the Guild ready for the next missions here."

Sulligan couldn't help but be disappointed by her decision, but she compromised enough by helping him uncover what was definitely some sort of hatch to what lay below. Sulligan always carried a small dusting brush with him on his missions, a reminder of what he planned to pursue in life once his Explorer's Guild missions were done. He brought it out from his pack and carefully dusted the area around the hatch. More glyphs, worn but still faintly visible, it was a language, he was certain of that now. He took more images to pass on to the linguists back home. This was his find, an alien language.

Chapter 6

The next morning, with the solar sail deployed, the shuttle began the long climb up the pass over the mountain range. Now that they had done some basic reading of the neo-metallic material that they had found, they fed the data into the shuttles on-board computer systems; the material no longer appeared on the screen as anomalies. Nothing out of the ordinary appeared on the nav screen and they proceeded at the shuttle's maximum speed to the top of the pass. Anya did keep Sulligan at the nav station as she manually drove the shuttle. She still did not want any more surprises. The camera and instruments were all running on automatic. All of this data they collected would be reviewed by others once they were back on Earth. The Miner's Guild always got the first look at the data. It was their continuous surveys and mining operations that kept the Guild expanding outward with each mission. Here however, she thought, would be a planet that would belong to the Archeologist Guild, with Sulligan the right man leading the effort.

From the top of the pass they looked down across another large plain. It was hard to tell if it was further down than the winding climb up. The plain was flat but for the distant horizon. A long straight gash in the land cut across in front of them. At first sight, it looked as if there was no way to get past it.

"I'm guessing three days to get to it," Anya said to Sulligan, using the magnification available on the front portal of the shuttle to get a little bit better look.

"A natural formation, a river maybe," Sulligan said.

"I'm not sure," Anya said. "It doesn't look natural. It appears to be cutting straight across, not meandering like a river. We will know more when we reach it." She stood up and stretched.

"We will have to find a way past it," Sulligan said, also standing up from his seat. "Maybe its shallow."

They both sat down again after their brief stretching and Anya gave her commands.

"It looks like a clear shot across to whatever it is. Max speed for now," she ordered Sulligan. "Command seat for me, nav station for you, imaging and readings will remain on automatic. We don't need any surprises before we reach it," she finished as she started up the shuttle again.

"The yellow brick road," Sulligan laughed as he took his station, trying to elicit a smile from his captain.

"The Miner's Guild certainly hopes so," she laughed back at Sulligan, breaking into a partial smile.

~ ~ ~ ~ ~

Amanda showed up unexpectedly at the farm, a home-made strawberry pie in hand. Anya had asked her to keep an eye on Gustof while she was away on mission. Gustof's dogs happily greeted her, their tales wagging. She had a treat for each of them.

Gustof still looked a little lost when she came up to the porch. At least he had cleaned up a little and had fresh clothes on. The friends from the pub had that positive effect on him when they visited the farm.

Gustof felt a little lost and uncomfortable with her in his home in its current condition. He cleared the kitchen table off, piling the dishes into the already full sink. Using a damp cloth he grabbed, Gustof wiped off the table and motioned for her to put the pie there. Amanda sat down at the table while Gustof put on a pot of the coffee (Anya's favorite) that they always kept on hand. The machine roasted, brewed and poured two large mugs of coffee automatically.

"Do you have any plates for the pie?" Amanda asked Gustof.

"Sure," he replied as he got two, oversized for the pie slices, clean plates from the cabinet. He then got two forks and a knife from the overfilled sink and washed them as Amanda watched with more than a little bit of concern for Gustof. 'The outing with their friends to the big rugby match couldn't be coming at a better time,' Amanda thought.

Amanda opened up the conversation as she places the two slices of pie from the tin onto the plates. With that Gustof sat down.

"I hear your buddies are taking you to the big match coming up," she said to Gustof, smiling.

"Yes," said Gustof quietly as he got back up again to get their coffee. He sipped from his cup as he walked back to the table. His thoughts drifted back again to Anya… and Sulligan. He worked to push out those thoughts as he sat down and handed Amanda her cup.

Amanda seemed to sense his thought as she looked at him. She took her own sip of the offered coffee. It was sweet as Anya always insisted.

"Have you heard anything about Anya's mission yet," she asked Gustof. "I hear it's a First Landing."

Gustof brightened up at that. "Just what I know in my heart," he answered. "She found something extraordinary, I know it," he smiled.

Amanda looked at his face and she could almost feel the connection that Anya and Gustof shared. She hoped to find that connection herself someday.

"What do you think she found?" Amanda asked Gustof.

"I know that it will change everything," he answered. He was sp proud of his Senior Explorer Anya. But that brought more thoughts of her alone with her apprentice, Sulligan; alone 6 months at a time. He appreciated Amanda and his other friends. He understood that they were only trying to help him. But sitting here with Amanda, that wasn't what he wanted. He wanted his explorer home with him, not on another mission with Sulligan.

Amanda could see the change in Gustof's face as he thought of his wife. She continued the small talk with him for about an hour as they finished their pie and coffee. She was able to bring a couple of short-lived smiles to his face; talking about Anya, the dogs, the farm and about the upcoming rugby match. Finally she saw that Gustof was all talked out.

As Amanda got up from the table to leave, Gustof stood up as well.

"Thanks Amanda, the pie was delicious."

"Well, the rest of the pie is for you as well," she said as she indicated the remaining pie on the table.

"Thank you," he replied as he walked her to the door.

Amanda walked to her truck with the dogs following. She gave each of them a treat from the truck once more and turned back to Gustof.

"Enjoy the match, Gustof," she called from her truck as she started to drive away.

Gustof gave a brief wave as she drove off. He felt mostly lonely these days, even more so for Anya after the brief visit of Amanda.

~ ~ ~ ~ ~

It was almost three days before they reached the rift. They had had to make several brief detours when more small anomalies appeared on the nav screen. Just natural formations, but it slowed them down when they went around them.

Anya slowed the shuttle as they approached the edge of the rift. They looked across it with the magnification of the front portals, both in their front command seats now. The radars range finder said that it was about two miles across here. From their vantage point they could not see the bottom very clearly and the radar was unable to give a reading on its depth. It looked natural, but the lack of any side passages to the rift disturbed her. She had been to the expanding rift valleys of Africa on Earth and the Grand Canyon in North America as part of her training and this was different. If this had been a river-cut valley there should have been tributaries feeding it with their own small valleys. Part of a continental rift, like in Africa, that could be, but it seemed to straight for that.

"What do you think?" Sulligan asked her.

"I wish I could get a good view of the bottom and how it looks from below."

"We could still use one of the recon drones here," Sulligan suggested. "It may not fly but we can use the catapult to launch it as far and high as possible over the rift. We can then collect valuable data on its way to the bottom. We can even launch a couple of them. I do not see very much else use for them on this trip. We should be able to control their decent a little bit as well, keep them from tumbling right away in a free fall."

The recon drone could be launched from the jet-drones catapult, but they would have to be loaded manually outside the shuttle. That meant another hour of using the portable breathers and another small waste of their precious air. At least the condensers were able to replace almost all of the air they would lose from the planets thin atmosphere. The Senior Explorer looked out over the rift from where she sat. They needed the data and she was not ready to use the last of the jet-drones limited range.

"Let's get it done," she said to Sulligan as they both walked to the back of the shuttle from their seats to prepare to go outside. "We'll launch two of the drones. We'll set up their controls so that each of them will be guided from our command stations. Recording and imaging will both be on automatic under the computer's control."

"It's a race then," Sulligan said to Anya, smiling. "The last one to the bottom is the winner."

"Bets on, Sully," she laughed back. "Loser makes meals for a week."

"Its on then, let's get them launched. I'll prepare the catapult if you set the controls on the drones. We should be able to launch them together."

The job was pretty straight forward, however it would take some physical labor to get it done. The planets gravity was slightly less than Earths and that would help. Before leaving the shuttle to prepare the launch, Anya moved the shuttle up to about ten feet from the edge of the rift. This would give them the room they needed to launch the drones and still give the catapult the range from the edge that they wanted.

Sulligan extended the catapult arms with his controls, the jet-drone positioned on it. Fortunately the jet-drone was still just in its loading position. They had to lift the jet-drone out of its storage place on the catapult to reach the recon drones. It was more awkward than heavy. It weighed seventy pounds on Earth, but was almost ten foot long. They carefully lifted the jet-drone and placed it on the ground next to the shuttle. It would actually be easier putting it back into place on the catapult's arm when they were done than the unloading of it was.

The recon drones were small, less than three feet across and four feet long. They weighed less than ten pounds each. They were stored in a rack below the catapults arm to one side of the jet-drone. Sulligan retrieved two of them and brought them around the back of the shuttle to where the Senior Explorer stood next to the catapult. Anya set the controls on each of the drones to manual control, connecting them to their command stations. Anya briefly thought of leaving the drone attached to Sulligan's station on automatic as a joke, but she thought better of it. This information of on the rift was too important. The catapult had a special fitting for the recon drones. The idea of using the catapult to launch the recon-drone was used once before by a First Landing mission by a Senior Explorer who had had the same idea as Sulligan.

Sulligan climbed up to the storage rack above where the recon drones were stored. From there he could load both of the recon drones on the arm of the catapult, one after the other. The catapult had a special fitting on the arm that he could place between the two drones. Up to three could be launched at a time.

Anya handed the recon drones up to Sulligan to load. He fitted the drones onto the catapult. Once they were both back inside at their command seats, they would launch the drones from the catapult, seconds apart.

Once inside they both took their seats and prepared to launch the drones. Anya brought the shuttle to the edge of the rift and turned it broadside so that the catapult faced out over the rift. She deployed her anchor, forward and aft. She wanted to be right at the edge of the rift to give the drones their maximum range, however she wasn't taking any chances of the weathered ground giving way underneath them so close to the edge. Both were strapped into their seats. The catapult arm now reached out over the edge of the cliff.

Sulligan turned to the nav station checking that all the shuttle's sensors and measuring equipment were set to the drone's frequencies. They did not know how long the drones would be sending them data and they were making sure that they were ready to receive all of it and that none of the data was lost. They each checked the manual controls of the drones one last time. There could be no mistakes. Each station showed a green light; ready to go.

"Did you fly any drones back at home?" Sulligan asked Anya.

"A few at the farm, it's something that Gustof and I like to do together."

"Well you're one up on me then. I haven't flown one since my second year at the academy. And even then I didn't pay too much attention to the training."

"Good luck, then. I look forward to your cooking," she laughed. Then she got serious. "Ready for launch?"

"Ready."

"Then go ahead and launch them."

The drones shot out over the rift in a high arc, their camera's working and sending a cavalcade of images back to the shuttle. Everything was set to receive as much data as the drones could send. They didn't know how long the drones would remain steady in the thin atmosphere, but they each hoped that they could control the descent of the drones on the way down.

Anya turned her drone to the right and Sulligan turned his to the left in broad circles. The cameras and sensors were working fine and sending their maximum load of information on a stream to the shuttle computer. The two worked hard to keep their shuttles airborne as they began their descent, picking up speed, that it turn helped them control the drones on their small wings. The shuttles large propellers tried to grab onto the air as they descended.

Finally, after a few minutes of fighting the props with her controls, Anya shut off the small engine on the drone. Almost immediately she felt better control of the speeding drone as it turned into a glider.

Anya glanced over at Sulligan and saw that he was having problems controlling his drone.

"Turn off the motor, Sully."

Sulligan's drone was starting to tumble and he shut off the motor on his. He struggled to maintain control. Anya's drone was on a steady glide path now, circling down to the bottom. They switched seats and Anya tried to steady Sulligan's drone, without luck. She thought she had it righted several times, using dives to gain speed and control, but finally she gave up. It quickly started tumbling out of control. All of its sensors and camera's continued to work as it fell to the bottom of the rift.

"Ill take over mine again, Sully," Anya told Sulligan as she got up to resume her command seat and control of the remaining drone. Sulligan was having trouble controlling this drone as well and reluctantly gave the seat back up to his commander.

"Does that mean I lost," he asked her.

"Yes."

Anya's shuttle recon drone continued to work as it flew on its glide path to the bottom of the rift. Finally, it reached the bottom and landed in a cloud of dust and small rocks.

The shuttles onboard computers cleaned up the rough data that both drones provided. This provided a clear image to the explorers of what it recorded. The rift looked natural, but it also looked like it was created in a single giant event. There were no signs on the bottom of a river that could have cut this rift. It's depth was over a mile.

The earth had rifts like this, produced over countless millions of years. The Great Rift of Africa was a good example of that. This was different. It was too compact, too new, produced in just a moment in the recent geologic past and only now beginning to erode.

The first images after the drones launch, at the peak of its arc, showed that the rift ended to the planets northwest in the distance. To the Southeast they could see no end to it.

"The drones gave us a lot of data," Sulligan said out loud.

"Enough I think," said the Senior Explorer. "And now we know which way to go."

"Do you think that this rift had something to do with the end of the civilization on this planet?" Sulligan asked.

"It might very well. I'd guess what we have found so far would lead to that conclusion. We will have to leave that to others to figure it out," she responded. "Right now let's go retrieve the jet-drone and head north. Let's go see what is on the other side of the rift."

"The Emerald City, perhaps," said Sulligan.

"Maybe, you never know," she replied smiling at the thought.

This was quickly becoming the Explorer's Guild's biggest find, ever. They just looked at each other as the shuttle began racing north after retrieving the jet-drone.

~ ~ ~ ~ ~

Gustof's friends arrived at his farm in the early morning to pick him up for the rugby match. It was a six hour drive to their overnight stop on the way to the stadium of their rival, The Downs, where the match was being held and they wanted to get their early. They didn't think much of The Downs rugby team. However, The Downs region had some of the best fish and chips on the coast.

They were in Mark's big truck; Phillip, Michael and Mark; plenty of room in it for the four of them, including Gustof and their gear. A second truck pulled up into the driveway after Mark's. That was Jack and his wife, coming by to take care of Gustof's dogs while he was gone. Jack liked dogs, they were OK to him. His wife, Lilly, loved dogs; she brought along both of theirs.

Gustof was cleaned up and packed for the three day trip and he met them all on the porch. When Lilly let her own two dogs out of their truck, Gustof's two dogs ran off the porch to join them in play. All four dogs raced across the field to chase the ground squirrels.

"Ready to go G," Michael called out to Gustof as the five of them climbed out of their trucks.

"All-ready," Gustof called back, trying to sound cheerful. He had had another rough night sleep; dreams of Anya and Sulligan together alone, dark thoughts of the two of them. 'Where are these thoughts coming from,' Gustof thought to himself. 'I trust them both completely, but…'

Lilly came quickly up the steps and headed to the door.

"I have to use the facilities, G"

"I'll set the door's security vibration current to you," Gustof said as he walked the few steps back to the door. "It's a mess inside."

"Just-hurry," she half-smiled as she hurried through the security screen.

"All set."

"Let's go, G," Michael called to Gustof. "The chips are waiting."

Jack was on the porch now as well.

"Just go enjoy the match. Lilly will take good care of the dogs. We have it here."

Gustof looked at Jack and then at the others waiting for him by Mark's truck. Jack was right, he and Lilly would tale good care of the dogs and the farm while he was gone.

"Just let me set your frequency to the security screen too. Go ahead and walk through, I'm ready.'

Gustof made a minor adjustment to the screen from its panel on the porch and then was done.

The security screen added Jack to its file as he walked through into the house. Jack took one look at the inside of the house and shook his head. The three of them, Lilly, Amanda and himself had their work cut out for them. Gustof needed them all right now, Amanda had been right about that.

Lilly rejoined Jack and then went back outside to the porch to wave good-bye to the four guys as they left.

"When is Amanda due?" Jack asked Lilly.

"She'll be here around noon. She will have to close the co-op early for the rest of the day," she answered.

"It's worth the inconvenience for us all. Did you get a good luck at Gustof and this place. He and his home were always immaculate. Something is definitely wrong with him."

"I saw that in his face," Lilly softly spoke. "I hope that we can all help him with what is wrong."

~ ~ ~ ~ ~

The rift narrowed as the shuttle headed to the planets northwest, drawing shallower as it closed. It took them another two days from when they launched the drone to reach the rifts northern most point. It didn't end in a narrow crack like they expected, but in a wide incline several hundred yards across. It looked as if some object had hit the ground here at high speed and low angle, plowing its way into the planets surface.

They could easily drive across the nearly flat area of debris where the object appeared to have first struck the planets crust, if that was indeed the case. However, they decided they would not head onward until they had done a thorough investigation of the ground surface of the rifts slope; collecting samples and studying the substrata with the radar to search for any anomalies.

"Once scared, twice prepared," she said to Sulligan. He drove the shuttle down to the crevice where it was less than a foot deep as she sat at the nav station, watching the screen and charting.

"Do we follow the slope down?" Sulligan asked Anya as they entered the slope.

"We'll follow it down a little ways. A lot of shadows down there and we don't want to run out of power. We'll go as far as the sunlight allows."

"This doesn't look natural, does it."

"No, Sully, it doesn't. It would be a narrow crack and steep valley here if this was a rift valley. I'll keep the instruments on full and keep recording as much data as we can." Anya thought for a second and added, "I'll also set the controls for the full spectrum of the periodic table and try to get any latent radiation readings; I have a hunch that just won't go away."

"A hunch, huh…"

"Yes, I wish I could see the other end of this."

"Maybe on the way back?" Sulligan asked her.

"Yeah, maybe…"

The force that created the cut in the planets surface was something that they had a hard time comprehending. It looked more and more from the data they collected that this happened in one titanic event. This was something the Miner's Guild would grab onto and explore. The amount of rare earth riches from this planets core they detected was staggering. She didn't think now that the miners would give this up to the archeologist without a fight. And she knew that the Archeologist Guild, from the language records that they had discovered, would put in a first claim for the planet. They had found more than enough riches for both Guilds on this planet and the survey had just begun. Sharing would be the key word here, something that neither Guild was prone to do. The Explorer's Guild may have to get involved in a planets future once more.

"How's the energy level, Sully," Anya asked her apprentice, a little concerned with how the shadows had started to overtake them as they preceded down the slope.

"Still over 80%, we should be OK."

"What do you think? Keep going a little further down before we head back up to the sunshine or turn back now."

"I'd say we turn back at 70% energy level. If we speed up going back we should be fine. We don't have to get completely clear of the shadows; the sail raises a good 20 feet above us."

"OK, speed up a little bit on the way down. Let me know when the energy reaches 70%. You can turn around then."

"Well do," Sulligan answered.

They were able to continue the downward trail of the rift for another hour before Sulligan announced that they had hit the 70% limit on the power. He turned around the shuttle at that point and began the speedy accent of the rift. They had already checked the surface on they way down so Sulligan didn't hesitate to put full power on the shuttles drive. The shadows continued to creep up the slope as they made their way up to the top and for a while they wondered if they hadn't traveled too far down the slope. Finally, after an hour, they started catching up with the creeping shadows and an hour later the sail was clear of the shadows and the power readings started rising again for the shuttle. Sulligan slowed down the shuttle at that point and they made their way back to the surface in another hour.

"That was a great job driving the shuttle going down into the rift. We got a lot more data from that. I'll take over now," the Senior Explorer said to her apprentice, trying to encourage him further.

The Senior Explorer got back into her command seat and once again took manual control of the shuttle's drive and they took a southeasterly direction from the mouth of the rift. No anomalies appeared on the nav screen as they raced across the flat and barren plain.

She had Sulligan remove the nav computers filters that they had installed for the neo-minerals of the ancient city they had briefly explored. Still nothing appeared in the nav-screens. No anomalies, nothing but the great expanse with a thick crust of salt.

Then it occurred to her. She had not thought of it at the time of the descent down from the pass. They were racing across the dead sea of this long ago doomed world.

"Mountains coming up on the starboard, still some distance off. They just appeared on the radars horizon," Sulligan said to his captain. "Not too steep, but high, there appear to be a string of them. Volcanic range, maybe."

"Islands," she said back to him. "What is their heading?" she asked Sulligan.

"Twenty-two degrees to starboard," he told her.

"Let's go see what we can find on top of those islands, Sulligan."

"Islands?" an incredulous Sulligan said.

"Yes, Islands of this planet's long dead sea that we have been crossing since we came down from that pass."

Chapter 7

The climb up from the floor of the sea to the top of this *island* was a gentle climb until the very end. The filters they had put in of the neo-metallic materials that they found at the ancient city archeological site where they had briefly stopped were still turned off on the nav station. The Senior Explorer was in her command seat manually driving the shuttle while Sulligan sat facing the nav station. Everything was showing clear on the screens, no sign of anomalies, just the thin layer of salt that they had been driving across for what seemed an eternity.

Edible salt compounds had been found on several worlds and while not a big money maker for the Explorer's Guild or the Miner's Guild, the salts had found a niche market among the gourmet chefs of the Earth and its two colonies; each brought their own unique off-world flavor profile to the chef's cooking.

Sulligan looked up from his screen and called Anya. She turned in her command seat to face him.

"Why don't we remove the filters we installed for the sea-bed? We are climbing out of the sea and may find something of that past civilization? Right now all I am picking up is the salt and some old calcium deposits, probably bone material of the sea life that lived here."

"That's OK with me," she said back to him and Sulligan turned on the filters. The nav radars sensors went crazy. There were anomalies all around them. Artifacts of what came before them lay in an immense array. They had entered a wide broad valley as they had climbed the mountain that was the *island*. It occurred to each of them at the same time as the sensors exploded to life; they had entered the harbor of a long lost port of the ancient civilization they had found so many intriguing details about already.

With each passing day, this world was proving its worth many times over to the Guilds. The Senior Explorer could tell when she looked back over her command seat at Sulligan just how much he wanted to explore this site like the last. There just wasn't the time or the oxygen to do so.

'This is my world,' Sulligan thought to himself. 'My home, the reason I joined the Guild.' She could feel his emotions without asking.

"I am sorry, Sulligan," she said as she looked back at him at the nav station. "I will make sure you get credit for this find when we report back to Earth. But we are just not equipped on the shuttle to do any more archeologist work and the range craft is not designed to bring back any more of your samples."

"Not even for half a day," he pleaded with her.

"This is already our third major archeological find. This is a significant world. Trust me, Sulligan; you will be a big part of the future of the exploration of this world."

He completely trusted her. He knew that in her reports back to the Guild she would prominently mention him. Anya held major influence within the Guild as the youngest individual named to be Senior Explorer. Gustof's work with the Guild on future food stuffs the Guild would need only enhanced that. And now, with these significant finds of great value to the Guilds, her esteem within the Explorer's Guild would be even greater. He would get his chance at this world. Sulligan was confident that she would make sure of that.

The shuttle slowed to a crawl as it traveled through the remains of this ancient port city. Anya in her command seat tried to cover as much of the site as possible in driving through the ancient city. Sulligan flit from nav station to the optical scanners to the sensor analyzer station and back. At one point he had her stop the shuttle briefly to get a detailed optical scan of another neo-metallic sheet, this time lying on its side, partially covered in dust. He increased the magnification of the optical scanner. He employed the nav's radar to try to get a cleaner look through the dust. It was covered in glyphs like he had found twice before. This time the glyphs were complete, if partially obscured by the dust. It was definitely a language or maybe two different languages on the same sheet. They had found three sites now, distant from one another. Did they have the same language? There were still many different languages on Earth. This would be a puzzle for the linguist.

"From the pictures of their language, can you make anything out of it yet, Sulligan?" Anya asked.

"Only that the glyphs in the images appear similar. I do get a distinct impression on this last sheet that there are two different sets of glyphs. There are some duplicate glyphs from the other site. About all

I can tell is that it is a language. The rest will have to come from the linguist when we get back to Earth. Hopefully I will be able to meat with the Archeologist Guild when we get back."

"I will make sure that you do," she said.

The Linguist Guild was an important minor chapter of the Archeologist Guild. Up to now, they had had little to do on the found worlds. Now, thanks to Sulligan, they would be able to play a leading role in the exploration of this world. They would want to take full credit for the language Sulligan had found. Anya would make sure that Sulligan received the full credit for the find. This would be his 'in' into the Archeologist Guild she thought to herself.

Only a month into the mission and already 4 major finds; the city they had spotted from the air as they landed (she would make that the headquarters for future missions, that would keep Sulligan and the Archeologist Guild at the forefront of this worlds explorations); the giant rift of recent origin that cut across the planet; the site in the mountains they had briefly explored where Sulligan had made the first initial discovery of the lost language; the 'island' with the another finding of the language, a great distance from the first. In addition, a fifth find, that the great salt plain they traveled across so much was once a great 'sea' or ocean.

They spent the night on the opposite side of the *island* from the harbor. The way back down to the floor of the 'sea' was much steeper on this side. They would wait until the morning to start back across it.

That night the two of them ate popcorn and watched the classic video *Lost Horizons*. Somehow, the movie seemed appropriate.

~ ~ ~ ~ ~

Gustof took the offered front seat of Mark's truck as they headed out to The Downs to see the rugby match between their team, the Seawolves and their arch rival, United. Phillip and Michael sat in the back seat.

They sat silently for a little while, while Mark drove. Finally Phillip spoke from the back seat to Gustof.

"G, how are you doing, buddy? We are all a little concerned about you."

Gustof just looked back at Phillip, not answering.

"You must be missing Anya a lot," Michael said.

"You know Gustof," Phillip said, "there are times like this when you are apart so long that the Guild created a special program for the spouse left here on Earth."

"I am fine," Gustof said back. "I miss here, but I am doing just fine." Gustof was a little bit defensive over this.

"Hold on, here me out. It's just a little program the Guild has where you can talk to others in the same situation as you are in. I didn't mean to intrude. We just want to help out friend."

Gustof turned to Phillip and looked at each of them in turn. He could see the concern in their faces. And he knew he wasn't right.

"Thank-you," he said to them all.

They mostly engaged in small talk the rest of the way and Phillip handed each of them a jersey and scarf to wear when they reached The Downs.

The Downs had a spectacular Rugby stadium that fit over 100 thousand fans. A lot of rugby teams in the area used the stadium, but usually the top half of the stands was typically closed to spectators. Not this time. The entire stands were open and the stadium was split in half for the match, Seawolves on one side, United on the other and the match was a sellout.

Gustof asked Michael how his own research was coming. Michael's specialty was molds and spores found in the ground, on Earth and its colonies. This was especially important to the Explorers Guild. Already one planet was closed to colonization because a dangerous spoor had been found.

"Work is going pretty good, G. I just finished up a new set of on a mushroom like plant species from a new explored planet that maybe edible for a new colony if one is put there."

"Wow," Phillip exclaimed. He was an engineer and mechanic who primarily worked to keep farm equipment in the area working. "What did you find out?"

"It looks promising as a food source. I can't find any harmful effects from it and it seems to have a high nutritional value."

Mark now joined the conversation. He was a short haul trucker and thinking about moving off-world. The colonies seemed to have everybody but the truckers they needed to keep things supplied and moving. He had already put in an application with the Colonist Guild subset of the Explorer's Guild. Anya had helped him with his application.

"Another colony would be a great thing."

"Yeah," said Gustof, the conversation once again reminding him of Anya on another world.

Mark looked over at Gustof from his driver's seat. He could see the change of expression in Gustof's face. He tried to change the subject.

"So G, what do you think our chances are in the cup? United has a pretty good team this year."

Gustof turned to Mark and answered him.

"The Seawolves will eat them alive."

That drew a laugh from everybody in the truck. This was the Gustof they were used to.

"How far to the chips place? I'm getting hungry," growled Phillip.

"About an hour," Mark answered. "Think you can last that long."

"If not I'll act like a Seawolve and gnaw off your arm."

That drew a laugh from everybody again.

They arrived at the pub in question inside the promised hour; that saved Mark's arm. All donned the team garb Phillip brought; jersey, scarf and cap. The pub was filled with Seawolves fans, although their waitress was wearing a United jersey; a good natured taunt aimed at all of them.

"So what you fellas want? You need to drown your sorrows before the match even happens tomorrow?" she laughed as she took their order.

"Fish and chips all around and two pitchers of Ale for my mates," Mark said back to her. "And you'll be the one drowning tomorrow."

"Are you going to the match," Michael asked, hoping to connect with the young waitress.

"Wouldn't miss it, arranged the day off over two months ago."

"See you there," Michael replied, hopefully.

"Only if you're sitting on the United side. The cup is ours for the taking this year," she said as she turned to get their order.

"Four platters of bottom fish with soggy chips, two pitchers of dish water," she called back in a way to make sure they all heard her. She walked away from the table, but not before giving Michael a second glance.

The other three looked a Michael.

"Not a chance," said Mark.

"Besides, she's United," Phillip added.

Gustof just stayed quiet and wished Anya were with him. He had more dark thoughts of Sulligan; that wasn't right.

Shortly the same waitress brought them the two pitchers of ale and four schooners.

"The chips will be right up. A busy night, the chef had to catch some more bottom fish for all of you Seawolves here."

As she handed Michael his schooner she also handed him a slip of paper before she quickly turned and walked away.

Michael opened up the folded note and read it to himself:

"Call me after the match. After the Seawolves
lose bad. I'll help you drown your sorrows."
— Julie

~ ~ ~ ~ ~

They raced across the bottom of the dry ocean bed. Sulligan had increased the radar scanner's range to search for more calcium deposits on a hunch. If this was indeed the remains of an ancient ocean there should be more remains of the life that swam in it. They had seen quite a few calcium hits on the sensor before they had climbed up the island. The hunch paid off.

Sulligan found a large singular calcium anomaly on the edge of the nav screen. He directed Anya to the site. It was the calcified boney remains of some creature that had lived in this sea in the distant past. While Sulligan took optical scans of the creature's remains, Anya used the shuttle drill arm to gather a sampling of the creature's bones. They would be able to get a DNA sample if they were lucky. And *luck was their lady* on this mission so far. She could not help humming the song as she worked the drill, carefully collecting a sample from the interior of the bones.

Her skill or lady luck, (sometimes they were one and the same for successful explorers the Guild had told her) stayed with them as they reviewed the remains they collected; it looked like they had found some ancient DNA from their scans. Lady Luck remained with them; this was a mission that would rewrite so much of what the Explorer's Guild and it's associated Guilds had learned. And she knew that they were not done yet rewriting the books.

~ ~ ~ ~ ~

Lilly and Jack arrived at Gustof and Anya's home in the early morning. Amanda would be joining them when she closed the co-op store early at noon. Jack turned off the home's security system like Gustof had showed him and called the dogs to him while Lilly went inside. She took a long look at the mess in the house and briefly wondered just what they had gotten themselves into.

"Jack, can you come in now and help. Laundry first, I guess, while I start in the kitchen."

"Oh, I'll be right in as soon as I feed the dogs. I'll check the greenhouse when Amanda gets here."

"Its quite a mess, honey," Lilly said as she looked around the interior of the house. "What happened, Gustof was always so tidy."

"I'm not sure," Jack said as he came in the door and looked over the mess inside himself. "Its more than just Anya being gone this time, I think. And he needs our help."

"Lets get busy then. After you get laundry started, could you run the vacuum?"

"No problem, hun."

~ ~ ~ ~ ~

All that they could see was salt, now deep, in all directions. Even the anomalies from the calcium had faded as they raced across the expanse that must have been at one time the deepest part of this ocean. Nothing to see or do for days, they would have to be careful, it was almost hypnotic. No changes on the horizon to break the monotony of the view. Had this planet been mostly ocean when alive? It now seemed probable.

As they raced across the expense that was this ocean bed, Anya had Sulligan take over most of the driving. She knew he needed experience driving the shuttle and she was concerned about some of the deeper depths of salt they were encountering. She didn't want them to get stuck in the salt and watched the nav radar closely for anything to avoid.

"I keep thinking about the movie we saw the other night before we headed back off that island. I think that we are going to run into the monster that hit the electrical field," Anya said and they both laughed.

"I keep thinking about the daughter," Sulligan said.

Anya just gave him a funny look and they both started laughing again.

The radars sensors were at their greatest range and they drove day and night trying to get across this sea of salt. They took turns watching the controls as the shuttle raced along on automatic. Eight hour shifts in their command seats at a time, eight hours to rest for the next shift. They ate their meals at the controls, doing anything to hurry this race across this expanse as quickly as possible. Not even *islands* were visible on the nav screens. Could it be that in the great size of this dry planet they were just missing things on the course they took.

Utilizing on his time away from the controls, Sulligan dedicated himself to studying the ancient language of the planet, trying to make sense of the inscriptions discovered on the scarps of metal he that they had found. It began to make some sense to him as he started recognizing more patterns. It was just one language he was now sure. Unfortunately, on the shuttle he had nothing to key it against to try to ascertain its meaning. That would take more time at the sites to find.

~ ~ ~ ~ ~

Amanda arrived just past noon and she brought lunch for the three of them. They all sat quietly on the porch for a few minutes while they ate it. Thoughts of what was wrong with Gustof were on all of their minds.

Finally Amanda broke the silence.

"How is it going inside?"

"Slow," Lilly said. "I am barely making headway in the kitchen. I'm really worried about G."

"I know," Jack added. " I have to go check the greenhouse after we eat. Have to make sure at least G's experiments are going well. I'll take the dogs with me."

"Into the greenhouse?" Amanda questioned.

"Yeah, the last time G took me inside and showed me the controls the dogs were with us."

"I'll help inside then," Amanda stated.

After finishing their lunch, Jack and the dogs headed to the greenhouse. The dogs trotted behind Jack; they knew their way. Jack opened the outer door into the supply room. Everything seemed in place here. Now a mess like in the house. At least that was a good thing. He walked over to the control panel that controlled the greenhouse's temperature and humidity. The air filter was next. Jack was a little surprised to see a little build up in that. The color of the dust it had collected seemed wrong, but that was hard to tell. Jack went back to the storage rack and grabbed two new filters and replaced the old ones. Both dogs were standing patiently by the inner door to the greenhouse.

"Ready to go in, boys?" Jack asked as he opened the door. The dogs entry into the greenhouse was part of Gustof's experiment on the affect of animals on the plantings.

Jack walked through the door with the dogs and approached the nearest of the raised planter boxes. He ran his fingers through the soil. It felt good in his hand and he loved the smell of the fresh earth in the planters. He walked slowly past the planting boxes, checking the irrigation lines, as the dogs raced ahead.

After a few minutes of looking over the planter beds Jack heard an unexpected noise. Both dogs were a few beds ahead of him and when he looked up he saw both dogs standing, front paws on a bed and their noses in the soil, disturbing it. That was something the dogs never did.

"What are you two doing, get out of there. Are you both trying o get me in trouble with G While he's gone?"

Jack hurried over to where the dogs were still standing on their hind legs, noses in the dirt.

"Down, now, both of you," Jack commanded the dogs. Jack half-pushed the two dogs back down and he gave a good look at the disturbed soil. Something had gotten the dogs attention. A mouse, maybe? As Jack looked over the disturbed soil in the corner of the planter box he saw something deep in the soil that the dogs had disturbed. The soil should have been a uniform dark brown color, but there, just barely uncovered, was a flash of orange-red.

"You definitely don't belong here," Jack said to himself.

Jack looked up and saw the dogs circling, almost dancing, around the next box as well. He walked over to it and dug his fingers deep into the loose soil there. Another large orange-red bio-mass was there. Now he was really concerned; this just wasn't right. He looked down at the dogs who were now just sitting at his feet.

"Good boys," Jack said to them as he realized the importance of their discovery. "Are there any more, go find them."

Not really expecting a response he got it anyways. Now having the scent of the spore the dogs rushed to the next box, and then to two more. Each time Jack dug his fingers into the soil and found more of the fungus bio-mass, each smaller than the previous.

"Just what have you found, boys? Does G know? Probably not or he would have never left on the trips with the mates. C'mon, lets get back to the house."

After letting the dogs all of the way back out of the greenhouse complex, Jack went back to the supply room, got a specimen box and collected a specimen of the fungus. "This just isn't right."

Jack carried the sample of the spore with him back to the porch and called Lilly and Amanda out. He showed the sample to them in its transparent plastic container.

"Have either of you seen anything like this before?" he asked them.

They only shook their heads, mystified.

"Definitely not native to this area or I would have heard of it," Amanda said with certainty.

"Do you think G know about it?" Lilly asked Jack.

"Can't see how he would have. He never would have left if he had known about it."

"Where do you think it came from?" Amanda asked.

"I have no idea," answered Jack. "I've helped G out a lot with his research. Its not part of anything I know of."

"We'll have to tell G when he gets back," Lilly added.

"Yeah, and give this sample to Michael to analyze."

"We're almost done inside. If you give us a hand, Jack, we can finish it up quick," Amanda said.

"Just let me wash up first. G has a good anti-fungal soap in his shop. I'll use that. Something is not right with the fungus."

~ ~ ~ ~ ~

Another week of traveling across the salt plains of this long dead ocean; they had traveled over half the length circumference of the planet. Just a few more *islands* appeared on the edges of the nav screen.

While they raced across the planets flat surface, Sulligan took his turns away from the command seat to work on his language samples from the distant past of this planet. It began to make some sense to him as he began to recognize more patterns in the glyphs.

While the shuttle stopped briefly for the mid-day meal, hash and applesauce, Anya announced abruptly to the startled Sulligan, "It's time to use the jet drone. One shot to see what's over the horizon. The only question is which way to launch it."

"We have been driving the shuttle on the planets North-South axis. that hasn't worked as well here as on other planets. I think East or West," Sulligan replied

"Your choice, Sully, which way is it? Let's find you another city."

"West, then," he said.

"West it is then," Anya replied. "A full load of fuel, we won't be retrieving it this time. Lets give it all the range we can. Set up a link between it and the station in orbit as well. We'll see just how much information about this planet we can gain with it."

"Any particular course that I should set?" Sulligan asked her.

"Just west for now, Sully, all sensors and camera's fully engaged and locked onto the shuttle and the station. Set all of the computers receiving sensors to full, we don't want to miss anything. I want manual override on the drone available. We'll follow its course to see if we need to make any changes. We'll spend the rest of day we have left watching the data as it comes in."

"Then we head for home base?"

"Yes, we still have some time left to explore the planet on the way."

The drone was deployed on the catapult and it was set for maximum, range and altitude with a steep climb rate. With the planets thin atmosphere they would have little resistance for the jet-drone and see more of the planet. However, the correspondingly high fuel burn rate would balance that out. This meant less air time and greater speed for the drone. They would have to keep a close eye on the data streams coming in to them if Anya expected to make any course changes.

For several hours, the picture showed nothing more than what they had seen for weeks. Had they chosen the wrong direction? The Senior Explorer moved to the remote pilot station of the drone to make a course change. The horizon was over sixty miles away at the height the drone was flying. The fuel of the drone was now almost used up the sensors showed, but this speed and height gave them the most coverage of the planets surface ahead of them. Another thirty minutes in this direction and she would change it to the south.

Anya got up from her command seat once the drone was launched and went back to the galley.

"Sully, do you want anything while I'm back here? I'm making myself a mug of coffee." She definitely needed the caffeine jolt to keep her extra alert right now. She had selected the coffee beans for the trip. They came from a small island off the coast of the Congo River delta and they were renowned for their high caffeine content as well as their sweetness and depth of flavor.

As she took her mug of coffee from the machine, she was called up front by Sulligan's excited voice. She grabbed his water bottle as she quickly moved back to the front of the shuttle, spilling some coffee along the way.

"What is it, Sully?" She asked as she handed him his water bottle and assumed her command seat, trying not to spill any more coffee.

"The drone has reached the edge of the ocean; another continental rise. Its probably the same continent we started our journey from," Sulligan said as he pointed to the steep rise from the ocean's floor he was watching on the video screen stationed behind them.

Anya was looking at the video screen where Sulligan was pointing.

"What the hell! What is… what was… what the hell was that," she more stuttered than yelled in a loud voice. Something had streaked across the continents rise. She had caught just a glimpse of it.

Sulligan just looked at her. What had she seen?

"Sully, can you reverse the images on the screen to where you just called me up to the front? About 5 minutes or so should do it. Them watch with me the upper right corner of the screen."

"The upper right corner, yes I can do that, but we will miss out on any real time data why we review it."

"We can catch up with that later. And full magnification of the video screen. I saw something for a moment; it was bright, shinny and long. But it was to quick a view to make out anything else."

"YOU saw what," he exclaimed, rewinding the imaging and increasing the magnification of the screen. "Are you sure?" Their eyes had plagued them with mirages as they had crossed the hot expanse of the dead oceans salt covered bed.

"I saw something and it was not natural."

Sulligan pointed to the video screen again. "Here it is, from where I called you up front from the galley. The jet-drone had just found the rise of the continent on the horizon. What the bajezus is that?" he now said as well and stopped the video screen. He reversed the video a few seconds at a time and changed it focus. There it was, unmistakable; long, shinny and torpedo shaped, racing across the sky, leaving a long jet trail behind it.

"We are not alone." Anya said quietly to Sulligan.

Chapter 8

They just sat in their command seats, Anya and Sulligan, almost disbelieving what they had seen.

"We are not alone, Sully," Anya at first just whispered to Sulligan, as if it was just a secret for the two of them. A moment later she jumped up from her seat, almost hitting her head on the shuttles ceiling. She shouted as she jumped up.

"Sully, we are nor alone! There's other life out there, we just saw proof of that." Her hands were shaking as she shouted. "We need pictures, Sully!"

~ ~ ~ ~ ~

Gustof was on the drive back from the rugby match when it happened. He just looked up into the sky and a giant smile overcame him.

"She did it. She actually did it."

The others just looked at Gustof and his smile.

"What did she do?" Mark asked.

"Do you mean Anya?" was Michael's response.

"Yes, Anya, my Senior Explorer, she just found something, something extraordinary. I can feel it, her excitement."

"What do you think she found?" Michael asked.

"I don't know," Gustof said a little sheepishly. "But I know that it will change everything.

Gustof's friends just looked at him again. They all knew of the almost ethereal connection that existed between Gustof and Anya.

"This will change everything," Gustof repeated.

~ ~ ~ ~ ~

After setting up every camera feed and sensor they had on the alien ship, Anya and Sulligan celebrated for about an hour, two good friends with an achievement that could never be taken away; *First Contact*. The future was theirs now, nothing was out of reach for either of them. One song after another played on the sound system from the

70 years of classic rock; the 60's through the 30's. Finally, they collapsed on the back bench, too exhausted mentally and physically to move. They sat that way while they recovered mentally.

"I need to retract the sail and reposition the catapult's arm," Sulligan managed to say as he staggered back to his command seat. "I'll have to go outside to do that."

"I'll give you a hand," Anya said as she got up as well. "We need to be quick about it."

"We see them, can they see us?" Sulligan questioned.

"I don't know. Bring the camera when we go out and we'll climb to the top of the rocks and try to get some more pictures of that ship. I think it's worth the slight extra loss of air. They're out there, someplace."

"What if they see us?"

"That's why we'll get the pictures on foot. Less chance of them seeing us here," was Anya's reply.

Together they retracted the solar sail and repositioned the catapult's arm for the night. Then they silently trudged to the top of the rocky bank above the shuttle, Sulligan with the camera in hand. As they approached the top they lay down and crawled the last few feet, trying to create as small a profile as possible. When they looked across the expanse of the dead ocean the cylinder was still there, circling the edge of the horizon.

"Its real, Sully, its real."

"That ship is huge," was Sulligan's rejoinder.

"Keep taking pictures. We need to record as much of this as we can. Try to get some perspective."

"OK, but only another 10 minutes, I'm getting a little nervous."

"So am I, Sully, so am I."

After another ten minutes of watching the alien craft and taking pictures they returned to their shuttle. After changing out of their suits, they both collapsed again on the soft bench seat in the back of the shuttle. Nightfall was almost upon them.

"I'll get us something to eat," Anya said to Sulligan after about ten minutes of silence between them as she made her way across to the small galley.

"Let's watch one of our old sci-fi videos," Sulligan called over to Anya.

"How about *Forbidden Planet?*"

"Yeah," Sulligan answered. "That's perfect and I never get tired of it."

Both fell asleep watching the movie.

~ ~ ~ ~ ~

Gustof and his friends returned back to Gustof's house late in the afternoon. He was feeling in a great mood after the match. Their team had crushed United, 45-12. They were surprised to see Jack waiting for them at the house. He was sitting on the porch with Gustof's two dogs and walked down from the porch to greet them.

They all bounded out of the truck, giving high 5's to each other and yelling loudly about the victory. When they looked over at Jack, all four could see right away that something was bothering him.

"I have something to tell you, G," Jack began. Not how was the match or anything was like that, just that he had something to tell Gustof. They knew something was wrong.

"Wait until we're all inside," Phillip said. "We're all bursting at the seems from the long ride." They all still wore their Seawolves jerseys.

As Gustof walked into his house he couldn't believe how cleaned up it was.

"You did this, Jack?"

"We all did."

"I can't believe how nice it looks. I left it a mess," Gustof said in admiration.

"Well I can't take all of the credit. Lilly and Amanda deserve that. It was their idea."

Gustof was now a little embarrassed about the house cleaning.

"It wasn't that bad, was it?"

Yeah, it was" Jack answered, "But we're here for you G."

They all sat down and began taking their turns in the bathroom; Michael first. Gustof's dogs missed him and immediately both climbed up onto his lap. He gave them both a quick rub around their necks.

"A good match?" Jack finally asked.

"A great one, we crushed them," Mark said. "And Michael has a new girl friend now," he added.

"What!" Jack exclaimed.

"She works at the restaurant where we had our chips at. She's a big United fan and they still have a date coming up."

Michael was coming out of the bathroom as he heard that.

"Its not that big a deal," he said, a little embarrassed. He wasn't a big ladies man. They all laughed at that while Gustof took his turn.

When Gustof came back out he said aloud, "Whose next?"

Phillip was the next to hurry in.

"Make it fast," Mark said.

Jack took Gustof by the arm and walked him into the kitchen. There on the counter was the greenhouse sample box with the reddish-orange spore sample.

"What is that?" Gustof asked, both surprised and alarmed. It wasn't anything he recognized.

"I found it in the soil in the greenhouse." Jack answered. "Or at least your dogs did."

"What is it?"

"I was hoping you could tell me," Jack answered.

"Michael, come over here," Gustof called. "Let me know what you think of this."

Gustof then turned to Jack once more.

"You found this in the greenhouse?"

"Yeah," Jack answered him. "There's a whole bunch of it in at least four of you planting boxes."

Michael and the others came over and joined the two men in the kitchen. Michael picked up the box.

"I've never seen anything like this," Michael said. "But by its color, it can't be good, contamination in your greenhouse?"

"Yeah," Jack answered for Gustof who stood in shock. "A lot of it."

Gustof now tried to take charge, at least a little bit. Contamination, it couldn't get worse than that.

"Jack, take me and Michael there. The rest of you stay here. I have to see what's going on."

~ ~ ~ ~ ~

Now that they knew which way to travel to reach the continent again the trip didn't take long. Three days of travel at maximum speed and they reached the long climb up from the bed of the ancient ocean. By now they weren't worried about finding anything dangerous on the seabed floor. However, they were very concerned about the alien ship they had spotted and the possibility that they could be seen by it.

They had lost contact with the jet-drone early in the morning after the launch. Their first thought was that the alien craft had done something to it. As they reviewed the last of the data stream from it, they realized it had just run out of fuel faster than expected in the planets very thin atmosphere. The last images they saw were of the very same area where they had made planet fall. Another accomplishment for them, a near complete survey of the planets completed between the shuttles travels and the jet-drones path.

Without the jet-drones optical scanner running in an orbital path they were once again limited in the optics to the horizon and a little bit more with the over the horizon radar. Every few hours Anya or Sulligan scanned the sky for the torpedo shaped craft; no sign on it on the screens.

The question lingered and gave both of them some anxious thoughts. Had they been seen? And what would happen if they actually encountered the life behind the alien craft; would they be friendly? They looked at each other several times with the same thought. They were defenseless. Would future expeditions need to be armed? They hoped not.

For the last day they had noticed a slight rise as they traversed the ocean bed. The final climb up to the continent from the oceans bed only took about half a day. The only real sign that they had climbed out of the dead ocean's floor onto what was once the dryland of the continent was the sensor reading; salt and calcium deposits were replaced on the sensors by the neo-metallic traces of the lost race of the planet.

"What do you think, Sully," Anya asked of her friend and colleague on the expedition. "We have another 6 weeks scheduled on this planet. Do we keep going or call it officially done and prep for our return? We can relaunch to the satellite anywhere."

"I keep thinking of what we saw," Sulligan responded, sitting back in his command seat. "We are not alone on this planet. Somebody else is exploring it as well. I'm afraid that we'll actually meet them. And then what? I don't think we are prepared on this mission for a real first contact with aliens, friend or foe. Are they explorers like us," Sulligan paused and took a deep breath, "or conquerors? Look at our own earth's history."

"That's why we have the guild's guidelines. Trade, that's always been our first and only goal. The empty planets have given us the resources to keep exploring."

"But that has always been us doing the trading; between ourselves. What if they want the world just for themselves, for the same reasons, its resources? We are just not equipped, friendly or not, for contact. You saw the size of their ship. It dwarfed us."

"That's true, Sully. None of our missions are armed. I guess that is just naiveté on our part. I'm not sure we ever thought we'd find somebody else."

"That's the point, Anya,. We never thought we needed a means of defense or a way to communicate. Everything we have found to now have been long dead. It has been one long dead world after another. We have never really questioned why there were dead worlds. These First Landings have been strictly to gain new resources for the Guilds to share. The Explorer's Guild word has been law, but now what?"

"I know Sully, I understand your fear. I feel it myself. I don't think anybody in the Guilds thought we'd ever actually run into anybody out here."

"It's you call," Sulligan told her.

The Senior Explorer wanted to stay. They had accomplished so much, already. And what if she was the one to make actual First Contact with another race of space-farers like her and Sully. Then her common sense kicked in, the part of her that made her a great Senior Explorer. She, they, were just not ready. New protocols had to be established and defense measures put in place; just in case the first contact went badly. The Guilds, especially the Explorer's Guild, were just not prepared.

"Sully, get a reading from the satellite. See if there is anything more on the incoming mass." She was more than a little concerned that it wasn't just space debris.

"The satellite is still tracking it. Still weeks away. It looks like it is just a cloud of rocks and debris."

"That's a relief at least. I almost feared that it was the mothership of the ship we saw."

"Like *Independence Day*."

"Yeah, just like that."

"The movie tonight," laughed Sulligan.

"Sure, why not. Anymore on the debris field?"

"Just that its still weeks away, mostly space dust and it should miss this planet altogether. The satellite will be safe. I'll set an alarm into the nav computer for any changes."

Anya looked over the latest scans from the satellite. Nothing there to cause an early return home by way of the long-range craft tied to the satellite. But no scans of the ship they had seen as well. Somehow it had been missed.

It was time to leave.

"Sully I'm going to put us into the shadow of that mountain. It will provide us some security from what we saw. Then we'll shut down everything but essentials for two days and go over everything we've discovered. After that we'll begin our return. Make sure the batteries are fully charged."

"Great," said the relieved Sulligan. "When we've reached the spot you've picked out I'll be ready to initiate the shutdown and get ready the analyzers. We have a lot of data to cover. Do you think that ship is manned? It seems to behave like a robot."

"Yeah, it does seem to have those characteristics. The Guild thought of remote robots in the early stages of exploration, but they just wouldn't provide enough data."

"Does that mean they have been here before?" Sulligan questioned.

"I just don't know, Sully, but that's a good question," Anya answered.

~ ~ ~ ~ ~

Jack led Gustof and Michael into the greenhouses. Gustof stopped and looked up to the sky for a moment before he went inside with them. 'She's coming home early,' he thought to himself.

There wasn't anything out of the ordinary in the greenhouse's store room. Everything was in order there and Gustof didn't see anything unusual. They kept the dogs outside.

"Not in here, G, in the greenhouse itself," Jack said as he motioned them through the inner doors.

They walked into the formal greenhouse structure and Jack took them to the middle row of planter boxes. He pointed out to Gustof and Michael where the dirt had been disturbed.

"The dogs did that?" questioned Gustof as they walked up to the spot. "They never jump on the beds or dig in them like that. Their presence here was part of the experiment; to see how the plants would do around animal life."

"Yeah, I know that," Jack said. "You told me that when you brought me in here the first time to show me your work. That's why I thought it was so strange, so I walked over to where they were digging. I saw something in the dirt as I shooed them down. I put my fingers into the soil there and found the spore, just below the surface. That's the sample I showed you in the kitchen."

Jack reached down into the soil and pulled up another piece of the spore.

"What the hell is that?" exclaimed Michael, looking at the fresh sample.

"That's not something that belongs here," Gustof said abruptly. "This is sterile soil and the plants grow from seed."

"I'm going to grab a few more sample boxes," Michael said as he briefly left them and went into the supply room.

"I think that there is more, G," Jack said, walking to the next planter box.

As they passed several more of the beds they saw more of the reddish-orange spore, now peaking its way through the top of the soil. No leaves were wilted on the soy bean stalks, it didn't appear to be affecting them, but Gustof knew that this could be disastrous for his research that the Explorer's Guild badly needed.

"Where did this come from!" Gustof angrily exclaimed aloud. "I'm going to have to report this to the Guild. This could shut down the project," Gustof shouted as he angrily pounded his fist into the soil.

Jack put his arm around Gustof and tried to quiet him down. The outburst wasn't normal for Gustof. Something was definitely going on. The match had helped but now Jack was clearly seeing that Gustof had changed.

Michael arrived and collected a sample from each bed.

"We have to get to the bottom of this G."

"Yes we do. My research, years of work, it could all be destroyed by this."

"How could it have got here?" Jack asked.

"I don't know, I'm so careful, I record everything."

Michael now joined in. He held six sample containers, each with their own piece of the spoor, collected from six different beds. They varied in size from small to large, showing the growth speed of the spores. Other than size they all looked the same.

"Could it have come from outside?" Jack asked.

"I don't think so," Michael stated matter-of-factly. "I think this was brought in. I have to find out just what it is at my lab."

Michael turned and looked directly at Gustof.

"Can you wait a couple of days to give your report to the Guild for me. I should have it analyzed and identified by then."

"Meanwhile," said Jack, "I think that you should stay out of the greenhouse. I think those spores have done something to you."

Gustof just looked at his two friends. They were right, he hadn't felt right in weeks.

"Yes, I can't see how a few more days delay will make things worse. And the spores, I haven't felt right in awhile now."

"Yeah," added Michael. "That orange-red color concerns me."

They left the greenhouse and carried the samples with them. When they caught up with Mark and Phillip by Mark's truck, the two could see the worry on the faces of the three that went into the greenhouse.

"What is it?" Mark asked.

"I don't know yet," Michael answered. "Can you take me straight to my lab?"

"Sure," said Mark, a touch of concern in his voice. "We'll put those in the truckbed," he added as he pointed to the sample boxes.

"Let's get G inside," Jack said to Phillip. "He's had quite a shock. I'll give you a ride back home."

"OK," said Phillip as he took Gustof's other arm and the two brought him inside.

All Gustof could do at that point is think of Anya and wish that she was there where he needed her.

Phillip looked at Gustof as they sat him down in a chair.

"You know G, one of us could stay here with you while we wait for what Michael results. How about it?"

Gustof looked back and forth between his two friends.

"Yeah, I guess so. That would help."

"I'll stay then," Jack said. "I'll pick up some things after I take Phillip home and come right back."

~ ~ ~ ~ ~

Anya looked up from her command seat. Something was wrong with Gustof. He needed her.

"Its time to go home, Sully."

Sulligan was more than ready too leave the planet and return. He had done all he could in the shuttle to analyze the languages they found and he found more patterns in them. He wished that he had studied more linguistics in school. He had already finished the shuttles checklist for the return to the satellite and begin the journey home. They had returned to the oceans bed for the take off.

The launch procedure for the shuttle's return wasn't much different than when they launched the drone. The shuttle's solar sail and catapult were retracted into place and the shuttles roof doors lowered over them. The shuttle's wings partially extended on either side and would fully extend outward once airborne. The shuttles wingtips, not used during the landing, would extend out from the wings once the shuttle reached its top velocity. They needed a long runway to get airborne, hence the return to the flat ocean bed. It would take over 3 miles on the flat plain to reach take-off velocity. Any bump could lead to a dangerous tilt in the wings; why they weren't fully extended until airborne.

As they started to accelerate on the planets surface, the wings narrow flaps now extended behind them for more lift; another of the wings features not used in the landing.

As the shuttle started to gain elevation Anya continued to increase the power of the shuttles jet engines to full. Once the shuttle was airborne and had reached a departure angle of 30 degrees from lift-off, the wings of the shuttle fully extended outward and then moved slowly to their delta wing position with the wingtips fully deploying upon achieving that.

As if they actually had a choice, both Anya and Sulligan were fully strapped into their command seats, ready to hit the emergency escape lever if needed- They both knew, however, on First Landings there could be no emergency escape. That lever was for future missions to the planet. From the orbiting satellite the shuttle could be refueled and refitted for future landings to the planets surface.

The G forces continued to increase on the two of them as they reached escape velocity; they expected to receive a full eight g's of force during the take-off.

"Two minutes to escape velocity," Anya tied to shout to Sulligan in his command seat next to her, barely able to get the words out. "Full velocity engaged."

With the planets thin atmosphere it took half the planets circumference to pass through the planets outer atmosphere and reach space. Once there, Anya changed to pitch of the shuttle to move it to the orbital path of the satellite station for their rendezvous with it. Both of them looked out the portal in front of them for the alien spaceship; no sign of it. They both breathed a sigh of relief over that as the shuttle jet engine shut down. They now used just the small maneuvering jets to approach the satellite.

As the shuttle neared the satellite, the satellites computers took over the shuttle and the shuttle did a 180 degree turn, the shuttle portals once again showing the planets surface beneath them.

Chapter 9

"There!" Sulligan shouted. "I see it again."

"What did you see?" Anya asked, looking up from her station on the satellite.

"I was looking through the station's portal facing the planets surface and I saw it."

"What, Sully?"

"A silver streak crossing over the oceans floor, not far from where we took off from."

"Norma," Anya called out to the orbital stations computer, "any sign of anything tracking us from the planets surface?"

The orbital satellite station's computer was more advanced than the shuttles and had voice recognition and response. Somebody at the Explorer's Guild had named the system Norma and the name had stuck.

"Nothing on the surface appears to be electronically tracking us. However, Commander, I have no way of knowing if we are being visually tracked."

"Norma, do you track the object in the planets atmosphere?"

"I am doing a visual tracking of the craft and a video analysis. Should I use our radar? The craft is going behind the planets horizon from us."

"Not at this time, Norma. Forward all video to our long range ships computer for our return."

"That computer's storage is near max. I can load the video onto a portable unit if you like. I carry several."

"Yes, do that Norma. And any data you have collected of that ship."

"It will be ready for your return flight to Earth."

Sulligan got up from his work station on the satellite. Their quarters were more cramped than on the shuttle, however, the computer had far greater capacity.

'Safe for now,' Sulligan thought to himself as he walked over to the beverage dispenser to prepare a drink. There was no coffee maker on the orbiting station.

"We need to leave as soon as everything is transferred to the long-range craft," Anya said to Sulligan.

"Agreed. I've already started uploading the photos and research logs," Sulligan answered.

"Have Norma transfer the shuttles video logs onto one of her portable drives, that way we won't loose anything."

"Good idea, Anya," Sulligan said. "I'll also have her transfer over to the portable storage the video I have already moved over. That will save room for most of our videos for the return trip."

"Even then, only upload the videos that we haven't watched," Anya half-laughingly said. "I will be moving the coffee-maker to the long-range craft; I can't go without that for six weeks."

"How about the popcorn?"

"Not much left, Sully. But I'll find room for what we have."

"Just have to ration it I guess."

~ ~ ~ ~ ~

It was three days since Gustof arrived back at his farm from the rugby match and Jack had showed him the infestation in his greenhouse. He was doing as his friends suggested, staying out of the greenhouse until Michael's report came back. He was sitting in an old rocking chair Anya had given him with his two dogs, impatiently waiting for the results. A mug of Anya's coffee, half-drunk, was in his hand. Gustof looked up through the window to the stars in the nighttime sky. Jack was asleep in the guest room.

"I miss you, Mrs. Branch. I'm starting to get better now. I love you." He looked up to where her star in the sky was as he said the last part.

~ ~ ~ ~ ~

Their time on the orbiting station was going to be short anyways; it wasn't designed for a prolonged stay. Now they worked to launch the long-range ship in the shortest possible time. The dust cloud continued to approach the planet, and while they would have to give it a wide berth on the passage out of the system, it would miss the planet by several hundred thousand miles. The bigger *threat* was the alien ship that continued to cross the planets surface beneath them. Whoever or what ever they were, they seemed to be engaged in a systematic mapping of the planet's surface. Anya and Sulligan had no idea if they had been seen. They had to assume that they had been.

"Their own first mission to the planet?" Sulligan asked Anya.

"I don't think so, Sully. My worry is what happens when they are done with the mapping they seem to be doing. So far they haven't bothered us. That could change."

"It could be just a robotic ship, just here to map the planet," Sulligan said hopefully.

"That could be, I guess, and it just doesn't have any commands to find us. I just don't know. The Guild originally had plans for robotic First Landings. That changed after they figured out the robotics would miss things. That could be the case here."

"I still want to get away as quick as we can," Sulligan replied.

"You and me both, Sully. Let's wrap things up here and get under way."

Anya finished loading a short-burst pulse message to Earth into the satellites comm. System. The amount of storage and power only allowed for a 15 second message burst. They would reach full communication with Earth in two weeks from launching their return flight. Anya had thought hard of what to include. It would be received in hyper-light pulses and decoded by the Guild. The problem was, anybody on earth could receive it. Or even anything in its path, as she now contemplated the fact that Earth was not alone. Anya thought hard of what it should say, finally recording the message to send.

> — Emergency return initiated.
> Three major finds on planet.
> Saw our mapping ship —

Anya hit the send switch on the panel, sat back in her command chair and smiled. She could only imagine the consternation it would be received with at the Explorer's Guild Headquarters. They would receive the message in a little more than a week. She would have to be ready for their questions when they came within communication range of the Earth through the beacons.

~ ~ ~ ~ ~

Gustof woke up in a jolt. He was sweating throughout his body. He felt the thought as if Anya was laying there beside him. 'We are not alone.' Just what had his Senior Explorer found? It was just past midnight and he wrote down the time in the notebook he always had on his nightstand. Gustof then walked out to the porch with his two dogs and sat down.

"What have you found, Mrs. Branch, what have you found?" He smiled a proud smile as he said these words to her star.

Michael arrived early the next morning with results for Gustof. Gustof had finally fallen asleep on the front porch chair, his two dogs on either side of him. It was the dogs barking that woke Gustof up as Michael drove in with his truck.

Michael hurried out of his truck and up to the porch to the rapidly awakening Gustof. He carried a stack of papers and his own laptop.

"I have it, G," he called out as he ran up the several steps to the porch.

"What did you find, Michael?" a groggy Gustof asked.

"The spore, I know what it is. Get me some breakfast and I'll show you inside."

The two men hurried into Gustof's home and then over to his kitchen. While Gustof got them sausage and eggs, Michael laid out his papers on the table for Gustof to see. He opened his laptop to his work as well. Gustof kept looking over his shoulder at Michael while he cooked the breakfast. Jack awakened to the smell of breakfast and hurried out of the bedroom. He saw Michael sitting by the table spreading out his papers.

"What did you find, Michael," Jack asked as he hurried over.

Michael looked up from where he was sitting at the table. He could see the anxiety on Jack's face.

"It's not local. It had to have been brought in."

"What is it?" Gustof almost pleaded as he filled all of their plates and grabbed utensils.

"That's what took me time to find out. It took every resource I had to find it. It's extremely rare and extremely dangerous to people."

"To people! How about plants?" Gustof asked.

"It's derived from a Congo River mushroom spore. It was an experiment that went extremely bad 20 years ago. They were researching memory loss. Instead they got what's in your greenhouse."

"How did it get there? Gustof questioned as he sat down at the table.

Michael paused for a few bites before he went on.

"This is good, G."

"Enough stalling. What is it? How did it get in there?" Jack asked.

"That's the thing. It had to have been brought in by somebody. It dies quickly outside of greenhouse conditions like yours. And the only known sample, outside of yours that we found, is in an Explorer's Guild facility in Greenland. Some researchers still think it could have benefits and it was stored in Greenland because it can't grow in the ice and cold of Greenland. It would die almost instantly."

"The Explorer's Guild, that makes no sense."

"Lets finish breakfast and I'll tell you the rest."

They were all quiet for almost ten minutes while they finished the breakfast that Gustof had prepared.

"Well," finally said as he put down his fork and washed down the breakfast with grape juice.

"There's a tie to the Guild," Michael started. "I know that doesn't make sense. So far I haven't contacted anyone there about it. That's why I finished my report on paper. Nobody will see it unless I want them to."

"What does the spore do?"

"It heightens certain sensitivity in people; paranoia, apprehension, distrusting others."

"My God," Gustof exclaimed. "That's what happened to me."

Michael got real serious then.

"Gustof, G, my friend," Michael said as he reached over and put his hand on Gustof's hand, "I am pretty sure that this was aimed at you and Anya."

"Anya, why would anybody…"

Jack interrupted him. "She or you, you both have accomplished a lot in a short time. Enemies can be made."

Gustof couldn't believe it. "Nobody would go after either of us."

"G, I am really worried. If we hadn't found it, who knows what would have happened to the two of you."

"But…But…," Gustof stammered.

"G, I put it all down on paper here; where it came from, the research, Greenland… everything. Do you know anybody in security with the Guild. We have to keep this quiet until we know more."

"Who could have done it?" Jack asked.

"It would have to have been a visitor here. You have your log books, G?"

"Of Course, Michael, that's a Guild requirement for my work."

"Good, those will have to be gone over."

"How long do you think its been there," Gustof asked.

"Not more than a few months," Michael answered. "It's a fast growing spore in the right conditions."

"Such as my greenhouse."

"Yeah, just like your greenhouse."

Gustof sat back for a moment in his chair. He finally spoke again.

"It's good that its only been there a few months. But that still leaves a lot of visitors. Every few weeks somebody from the Guild comes by to check on my research. In fact, they are due this next week."

"Is that somebody you can trust?" Michael asked Gustof.

"Yes, he's been coming by every couple of months since I began the project three years ago."

"Gustof," Michael spoke in a solemn voice now," call me when he comes. I'm keeping the samples in my lab for now. I'll bring them when he comes. Meanwhile we keep this between the three of us, don't tell anybody about this."

Michael paused for a moment. "I'm afraid for you G, really afraid."

"OK, Gustof said, shaking in his body at the thought of sabotage aimed at he and Anya.

He thought of Anya right now, them holding her each other in the morning and their feelings of protecting each other.

~ ~ ~ ~ ~

Sulligan had finished the long-range craft for the journey home. The uploading of the satellites files to the crafts computer was done as well. They would need every bit of storage in the long-range crafts storage system for everything they had seen and discovered. There was a lot of data they would have to leave behind. It would be collected and studied on a return trip by the Guild.

They were ready for the 6 week return trip. Anya thought briefly of Gustof and smiled. She'd see him again much sooner than expected.

Sulligan had the satellite stations visual system following the unknown craft as it circled the planet below. Three more times it came within visual range of the satellite. They made no attempt to communicate with it. The ship was definitely on a mapping mission, each pass across the planet was on a different line. They still had no idea if the ship was robotic or manned.

The satellite picked up what appeared to be a transmission from the strange ship; however almost none of it was intelligible to them. They loaded the partial transmission into the storage of the long range craft's computer storage and they were ready to go.

"Time to leave, Sully," Anya said as she shutdown the satellites operations to a minimal orbital level in preparation for the Guilds return. They decided to have the satellite go dark as far as its instrumentation went; less chance of it being seen by the ship below. Both of them argued the point with the other on whether they had been seen by the ship. It was a mute point, anyways.

Were the aliens as leery of them as they were of the aliens? There would be more, much more, to be considered, on the return trip to this planet. If there would be such a trip. It was a rich planet and worthy of a return, however, was the Guild and Earth ready for a true first contact, which seemed likely if the Guild chose to do so.

Sulligan was already aboard and seated in his command seat when Anya made her way though the tube that connected the satellite to the ship. She manually checked each control on the short passage. Once in her own command seat on the long-range craft, she ordered Norma to disengage the tube, retract it and go silent until the Guild returned.

Their umbilical cord to the station broken, Sulligan used their crafts small thrusters to move to a safe distance from the orbiting station.

"Ready for return, ready and anxious."

"Then lets go. That was a First Landing for the ages."

The long-range crafts engines engaged and they were on their way home.

~ ~ ~ ~ ~

The brief message from the Senior Explorer was received back at the Guild's Mission Control. It immediately created a stir. Just what had the message meant? Another mapping ship? Contact, or just the remains of another planet's visit there. It would be another two weeks before they could learn more. For now, the only official notice would be that the expedition would return three weeks earlier than planned after a successful mission.

~ ~ ~ ~ ~

A week later Gustof received a call from Max, his friend from the Inspector Generals office. He would be by in two days to look over Gustof's work. Gustof immediately called Michael to let him know.

"I'll be by first thing in the morning," Michael told Gustof.

"Bring your findings and the samples," Gustof reminded him.

"I will."

Max arrived mid-morning in his truck. He wasn't expecting anything more than a routine review of Gustof's greenhouse project and a quick perusal of his logbooks. When he got there Gustof and Michael were sitting on the front porch waiting for him. Gustof motioned Max inside and they walked in together. That was unusual and caught Max's attention right away. They usually just walked over to the greenhouse and did the review there.

The first thing that Max noticed was the clear sample case that Michael was carrying with the large reddish-orange spore inside. He recognized Michael from the lab work that he did for the Guild.

The three of them sat down around a table that Michael set the sample box on and all three were silent for a few minutes. Michael pulled his report out of the briefcase he carried with him. Max just looked back and forth at Gustof and Michael, waiting for one of them to speak. Finally Michael broke the silence.

"Max, I'm glad you're here. We found that in the greenhouse," Michael said, pointing at the sample case.

Max looked directly at Michael.

"What is it?"

"It's a rare spoor, originally from the Congo River basin."

"Where did it come from? Why is it here?"

Gustof spoke now, painfully, "It's been in the greenhouse for weeks. We just found and identified it this past week."

"You should have notified the Guild when you found it," Max began. "It could be dangerous," Max stated, surprised that it hadn't been reported.

Michael spoke up now.

"It is dangerous; it's a hallucinogenic that causes paranoia. And it came from the Guild."

"What!" Max exclaimed.

Gustof started speaking again.

"It could only have been brought here by somebody with Guild access."

It was Michaels turn.

"We couldn't trust that the wrong people would discover what it is we found. It's only dangerous to humans and it won't affect the plants in the greenhouse. And it's only found in a Guild facility in Greenland."

"A Guild facility, it only affects people," Max was incredulous. "That means it was aimed at Gustof or Anya."

"Yes," Gustof solemnly said.

"That's why we waited for you," Michael added. "Here are my reports."

Max took the reports from Michaels hand and started going over them. Occasionally he looked up at Michael or Gustof and then went back to the reading. Finally Max looked up from his reading and spoke to the other two sitting there.

"Gustof, can you get me a mug of Anya's coffee?"

"Sure," Gustof said as he stood up and walked to the kitchen to get the coffee.

Once Gustof was in the kitchen, Max quietly spoke again so that just Michael could hear him.

"This is serious, Michael. You say that it's only at the Greenland facility?"

"Yes, I have a friend there I could trust when I was trying to identify it. The spore cannot exist in sub-freezing conditions, in that environment. It's derived from the Congo spore, but there are some genetic changes they did to it. They think that it can have some positive benefits and uses so they keep the spore there. Even if it escaped the lab, it would quickly die in the freezing cold there."

"And somehow it ended up here, in Gustof greenhouse. It must have been a targeted attack then, not aimed at the research, which it wouldn't harm, but at Gustof or Anya."

"Yeah, that's what I figure," Michael answered.

Gustof returned with a mug of coffee for each of them, and after setting his mug on the table, handed Michael and Max their hot mugs.

"Well?" asked Gustof.

'Gustof, this is very serious. I need to see your log books, now! Are they in the house or the greenhouse?"

"They are right here. I brought them in when Michael closed up the greenhouse to me."

The spore was really affecting Gustof," Michael spoke up. "He was getting very anxious and paranoid."

"Any sign of it in the house," Max asked Michael.

"No, its not humid enough for it to survive here."

"I would think it would have been hard to transport," Max questioned.

"Not really, just keep it next to the body in a warm pocket."

"Well that is a concern. At least we are safe from it here," Max said. "Gustof, can I stay here for a couple of nights?"

"Sure, I have a spare bedroom you can use. Jack just left yesterday after staying with me while I began to recover. Why?"

"I want time to go over all of this," Max said, pointing at all of the documents and research Michael had prepared. "And I have a friend in security I can trust about this. I'll have her come here, a routine visit to see your work first-hand, Gustof. She'll believe that, she's wanted to meet Anya and you."

"Then what?" asked Michael.

"When she gets here the four of us will meet. Then we'll show her everything. This is going to be a real issue; the secrecy. I imagine she'll want to run the investigation from here."

"Here?" asked Gustof.

"Yes, for now you need protection. And Anya will when she returns."

"She found something huge out there," Gustof quietly said.

"What, how do you know?" quizzed Max.

Michael answered that. "He has a logbook of their connection. He knows every landing time, everything. The have some sort of physic connection." Michael finished the last part with a friendly laugh.

Max just looked at Michael.

"Do others know of this?" Max asked.

"It's just between the two of us and a few friends," Gustof said defensively.

Max leaned back in his chair and looked briefly at the ceiling before talking.

"That could be it, or professional jealousy or even your work here, Gustof. We just don't know."

As they all now sat back in their chairs a quiet descended over the room.

"This is between us," Max said the unnecessary words aloud.

~ ~ ~ ~ ~

The return trip to the earth on the long-range craft turned routine very quickly. They both worked hard to study what they had found on the planet. Anya focused completely on what she could find out about the unknown vessel they had seen circling the planet. She had a thousand conjectures about what it was and what it meant and dutifully wrote them all down. In the end she became convinced the ship itself was just a robotic reconnaissance ship. And that meant somebody else had their sights on the planet. It would be up to the Guild to decide what to make of her conjectures and what to do next.

Sulligan focused on the lost society of the planet and the language(s) he had found, discovering more patterns to the characters. It was starting to come together; a single alphabet with maybe 50 characters. However, context was the big issue here. He could collect all the groupings of the characters he found, but without context they were just meaningless gibberish.

At night (it was important on the long range missions for the crews to maintain a daytime/nighttime cycle) they would put on a video from their collection of classic videos. Their focus had now shifted completely from detective mysteries from the noir era to science-fiction; especially about first contact. They tried to ration what little popcorn they had left, but that was difficult.

In ten days they would be in long-range communication with the Guild's Mission Control through the first of the relay stations they had placed in space during their trip to the First Landing planet. Ten days and Anya hoped to have some more information for the Guild.

~ ~ ~ ~ ~

It was almost a week before Max's friend, Ashe from Guild Security, arrived at Gustof's home. Max had taken some of his vacation time to avoid any scrutiny of his time. Michael picked her up at the regional airport and drove her to Gustof's home where Gustof and Max were waiting. So far the cover was holding; Ashe was just taking some time off herself so that she could be introduced to Gustof and meet Anya later.

Gustof and Max were seated in the front room when Michael and Ashe arrived. Max arose and introduced her to Gustof. After they were all seated again and each held a mug of Anya's coffee, Ashe spoke.

"This is all very cryptic, Max. What's this really all about?"

Ashe glanced over at the sample box on the table; it now just contained the remains of the now dying spore.

"Is that it?" she asked.

"Yes," Max answered. "We've had to keep this quiet, not the usual channels. That…," he pointed at the spore, "came from a Guild facility in Greenland."

"And…?" Ashe asked expectantly.

"It's a rare spore that only attacks people's minds; a dangerous hallucinogenic," Michael stated.

"Is it safe here at the table, even inside that box," Ashe asked.

"Yes it is," Michael calmly said. "It's dying in there. It takes a warm and humid climate, like Gustof's greenhouse, to grow. That's why it is only stored in the Greenland facility."

"Ashe," Max said with a sense of urgency. "It was placed in Gustof's greenhouse. We think it was aimed at Gustof, Anya or even both of them"

"And it came from the Guild itself, you're sure of that?" She questioned the men, a serious look now appearing across her face.

"Yes," Michael reiterated, "from the Guild's own research facility there. My friend in the research center there said all known specimens of the spore were held there."

"How could it have gotten here then?"

"That's the point, why you are here," answered Michael. "Somebody who visited there stole a sample, it would only take a tiny bit, and brought it here. They could even have used a plastic bag in a pocket with a pocket warmer to carry it into Gustof's greenhouse."

"The point is," Max said, "somebody visiting that research center must have stolen it for one purpose; to bring it here. And that means a Guild researcher."

Gustof now spoke again. "I do have the occasional visitors here. Fellow researchers from the Guild. I log them all into my logbook. But I can't believe it was one of them."

Max started up now. "I have looked over the logs. Besides Gustof and Anya's friends, and we can cross them off, none of them had been to Greenland, there are just a handful of suspects. I can give you the list, Ashe."

"That helps. I have the clearance to get Greenland's log as well. I'll have to think of an excuse to go there myself. Maybe they haven't had a security review in awhile. It appears to me they need one. I'll have to tell my boss though."

"Can he be trusted?" Gustof asked.

"If he can't, nobody in the Guild can be. But I'll ask that he keep it secret for now."

Ashe looked over the names on the list.

"Are you sure that's all?"

"Within the time-frame Michael gave me, yes," Max answered.

She looked at the names one more time.

"I'm off to Greenland then. Max, just like you thought, we need to keep this between us here in the room."

She was speaking to Max but she was looking at Gustof and Michael as well.

"Max, can you stay here another week," Ashe asked.

Max looked over at Gustof who nodded his head.

"Yes, it will just be another week of vacation for me. I had too much of it saved up anyways. And I hear the fishing is great here."

"Wonderful," Ashe finished. "I'll be back here inside a week. Michael, can you take me back at the airport. It's best I don't linger here too long. Our suspect may return."

"Sure," said Michael as he got up.

"How about lunch before you go," Gustof said to all of them. "I can whip up something quick." Somehow Gustof felt safer with Ashe there and he really didn't want her to leave.

"OK," Ashe said, "but I want to head out right after."

"Lunch it is then," and Gustof went to the kitchen to work preparing their food with Michael's help while Ashe and Max went over Michaels reports together.

Chapter 10

Gustof saw the messenger from the Explorer's Guild sitting on his porch when he returned from his fields in the early afternoon. He didn't know what it meant, but his heart seemed to skip a few beats as he approached his home. Bad news; he shook that off. Gustof would have known if something had happened to Anya, they had that connection. 'So what could it be?' Gustof thought to himself. This was the first time that an Explorer's Guild messenger in his uniform had visited his and Anya's home.

The messenger stood and waited at the top of the steps and Gustof took the last few steps up to the porch.

"Gustof Taszko," the messenger said.

"Yes," Gustof expectantly replied, his hair and clothes dirty from working a new field.

'How in the world did *this* man manage to marry a Senior Explorer,' the messenger thought to himself. 'A land rat if there ever was one.'

The messenger began talking to Gustof in a gruff voice.

"I have news on your wife's expedition," the messenger told Gustof.

"News," the bewildered Gustof stammered.

"News and a request," the messenger continued.

"A request?" Gustof answered as he started walking inside to get cleaned up. The messenger followed him inside.

"Please clean yourself up and prepare to leave with me to the Guild Headquarters. Your presence is both requested and demanded."

"Requested at the Guild? My farm and dogs, I just can't leave them, demand or not."

"You are to set your equipment to automatic. You will be gone up to a month."

"My dogs!" Gustof exclaimed. "I can't just pack up and leave."

"The Guild has already been in contact with your neighbor, Jack. He was informed of the situation. Your dogs and your farm will be taken care of during your absence," the messenger said. "Now please prepare yourself for your departure."

"Why?" asked Gustof, still not comprehending the situation.

"I am only at liberty to state your wife, the Senior Explorer on her First Landing mission, has initiated an early return."

"Is she safe, is she OK? Gustof pleaded for answers from the man. "Why send for me?"

"Please prepare yourself for the trip. Clothing will be provided for you at the Guild Headquarters. Any other needs you have will be furnished by the Guild as well. Time is imperative right now. A Guild air shuttle will be here within a hour to pick us up."

This was news for Gustof. For the Guild to send a shuttle here, that was unusual. What was this about? Gustof stumbled into his bathroom. He looked at himself in the mirror and saw the mess he was. 'She couldn't see him like this,' he thought as he started to clean himself up; a shower, shave and he'd use the automated cutter on his hair. She was coming home early, that was great news. But why was he being brought to the Guild? That had never been done before. First Landings sometimes ended early and he knew she had found something pretty significant. That could be it. However, Gustof thought not. 'Just a cover,' Gustof said to himself. 'It's the investigation."

~ ~ ~ ~ ~

The long-range craft would be in communication range of the Earth in two days. Almost two weeks had passed since Anya had launched the early return from the First Landing mission. Two weeks to study the fleeting images of the unknown craft by her. For Sulligan, he continued his study of the ancient language(s) he found. He was trying to make some sense of the character groupings he was finding.

They needed to have something prepared for their next message home. The message could be fairly long this time and it needed to be complete. They could expect a response back in three days from when they sent the message.

Finally, after a lot of back and forth between each other on the message, it was prepared.

  — Planet charting complete.
  Dead civilization found.
  Planet has strong resources.

> Written language discovered,
> Working on its meanings.
> Cosmic debris cloud passed near station.
> Primary mission site noted.
> Distant contact, alien life confirmed.
> Images being studied. —

They both knew that last part would bring consternation and a lot of questions from the Guild.

~ ~ ~ ~ ~

Gustof's last sight as the shuttle took off from his farm for the Guild's Headquarters was Jack arriving to take care of his dogs and the farm.

When Gustof arrived at the Explorer's Guild Headquarters he was immediately escorted to an apartment complex where he was moved into Anya's home when she was at the Guild. As a Senior Explorer she had been given a large apartment to live in rather than the dormitories the Explorers and Apprentices used when they were at the Guild Headquarters.

While Gustof was certain that Anya was safe, he was still concerned about his being brought to the Guild's center of operations without any word of why. He knew within himself that she had found something big. But why the secrecy? They had planned on her rejoining him at the farm upon the mission's completion, not him joining her here.

As Gustof entered Anya's apartment, waiting for him there was Ashe. She waited patiently for him to sit down.

"How are you doing, Gustof? I am sorry for the subterfuge to get you here. Anya is fine. She's made a tremendous discovery."

"That's a relief, it's about the spore then," Gustof said.

"Yes, and we had to get you here as quickly as possible so that you'll be safe."

"Safe?"

"I don't have all of the particulars right now, however," she paused, "you were the target."

"Me?"

"Yes."

"We want you to send Anya a simple message from the Guild Communications Center. Just to let her know you are alright."

"OK, I guess," he told her. He wrote down a quick note on a notebook Ashe handed him. "Here it is."

"We'll send it with the next message to her return craft.'

"Thank-you."

~ ~ ~ ~ ~

"A movie and popcorn?" Sulligan asked Anya, trying to get her to take a break from studying the video of the strange craft. Almost wingless, it seemed much larger than their own shuttle, station and long-range craft combined. And it was built for flight. It was fast, circumnavigating the planets surface in about 14 hours. It seemed the question still to be resolved was, was there life in it or was it robotic. Sulligan thought that their had to be intelligent life on board while Anya was of the opinion that it was robotic. In her mind, if there had been someone onboard, they would have been spotted and the craft would have moved to find out who they were. A robot following its program would have ignored them for further instructions. It was Sulligan who brought up, maybe they were just as leery of first contact as the two of them.

"What was that, Sully?" Anya responded distractedly to him. "A movie, we have too much work to do."

"It can wait for now. My mind is getting clouded from studying that language. And you're not getting any closer to the secrets of that craft right now," was Sulligan's answer. "It's time for a break. It will be at least another day before we hear back from the Guild."

"What did you pick out from the library?" she asked him.

"A 1960's sci-fi classic. It seemed appropriate; *The War of the Worlds*."

""OK, Sully. You get the popcorn ready. I guess we could both use a break from our studies."

They both fell asleep before the movie finished. Anya's dreams were filled with images of the mysterious craft and of what the aliens must look like.

A day later they received the follow up message from the Guild. Three lines, that was it.

> — Send no Guild related messages.
> Personal messages only.
> Gustof at Guild Headquarters. —

Anya was shocked to see the last part. Gustof at the Guild offices; just what was going on.

"Seems like we created a stir, Sully," Anya said.

"Seems like it. No Guild business? What does *that* mean?" he answered back, reclining in his command chair. "The Guild must be concerned about what we've found."

"Alien race, evidences of a long gone race; don't know how much time we'll have to ourselves," said a concerned Anya, thinking about why Gustof would already be at the Guild Headquarters.

"At least Gustof will be there for you," Sulligan said, smiling for his Senior Explorer.

"It seems strange," Anya pondered. "Guild business with Gustof I guess. He does research for them. And I am looking forward to being with him again. It just seems strange, the timing."

~ ~ ~ ~ ~

Gustof was escorted into the Guild's Security Center early in the morning towards the end of his first week at the Guild's Headquarters. He was pretty much left to himself the first few days. He did have a Guild escort with him almost continuously and a Guild security agent stationed outside his door. By the third or forth day it became clear to Gustof that the Guild was protecting him. 'Was it that bad?' he thought.

As Gustof was brought forth into the Security Center he was greeted by the director. By this time he was no longer concerned about Anya. If he was to believe the whispers, what Anya had found would forever change the direction of the Guild.

As Gustof entered the Security Center he had to pass through several layers of security. Ashe greeted him as he passed through the first. At the final security station his Guild identity pass and the presence of Ashe wasn't enough.

"Don't be alarmed," she quietly spoke to Gustof as she walked up to the retina scanner. "I'm taking you directly to the Director of Security, Commander Skarieber. He's taken personal charge of the investigation. This is huge, what you uncovered. Much bigger than we first thought."

Gustof put his eye to the scanner and a light above it blinked green.

"What would have happened if I hadn't passed the test here?" Gustof jokingly said.

Ashe turned to him with a stern look on her face. "I would have shot you," she matter-of-factly stated.

"Shot me!"

"Just a stun shot. The security then would have taken you away to find out who you really were. Few people are allowed into the inner sanctum of these offices. And with what you uncovered, we are being extra diligent about your security."

"Why me, why am I needed for this investigation?" Gustof quizzed her.

"It's mostly to keep you safe until Anya is Earthbound again. Like I said, the spore was just the tip of the iceberg. This has become and 'eyes only' investigation."

"Have you found out who brought the spores?"

"Once we are inside. I've already said too much outside," she answered.

~ ~ ~ ~ ~

—I love you, Mrs. Branch.
Linguistic's Guild awaits your return.
End of message —

Anya saw the message from Gustof in the communication from the Guild. It meant a lot of Anya and communicated so much. Like their own secret code, it told her Gustof was fine and he knew she had accomplished a lot.

"Any message for me?" Sulligan asked Anya.

"Just routine, except for Gustof's message. The Linguistic's Guild is looking forward to your findings."

"You call that nothing, wow!"

"I don't know which of us will be busiest when we come out of quarantine," Anya replied.

"I have a short transmission to send," Sulligan said, getting up from his seat and stretching. "Still no official business on the channel?"

"Yeah, Blackout both ways, just personal messages."

"I guess it will have to wait," Sulligan responded.

"How is the inventory coming?" Anya asked her partner. "We want to have that done before we arrive. Our departure was pretty hectic when we left the station, I'm not really sure what we loaded."

"I'm going to the last storage area now. A lot of big stuff we put there."

Sulligan started walking to the back of the ship talking aloud to himself, "The Linguistics Guild, wow!"

Anya sat back in her command chair again, looking over the videos of the alien ship, a mug of coffee in her hand. She started daydreaming about Gustof and the Oak Tree. There wasn't much for her to do now until they reached Earth's orbit. As she leaned back in her chair, thinking of the two of them sitting under the oak tree, a sudden thought came to her head; Gustof, something was wrong; light-years away and she could still feel it. Anya abruptly stood up and looked around her. There wasn't any doubt; the connection she had with Gustof was very real. Her Mr. Branch was in real danger, somehow. She started to tremble and sat down.

"Sully, come here," Anya called to her apprentice. "Something is wrong."

"What," Sulligan shouted back, turning away from his work in the largest of the storage cabinets. "What's wr...." He didn't finish the statement. As he turned he slightly dislodged a large sample of the planet's lost civilizations architecture with writing on it.

Anya, facing the back of the ship as she stood, saw it happening.

"Sully, look out!"

Too late, as the large slab fell off of its shelf, striking Sulligan on his the side of his head and. Shoulder. He was bleeding from the wounds.

"Sully!" Anya shouted as she rushed toward where Sulligan lay collapsed, the slab laying to one side of him.

Anya kneeled over the unmoving form of Sulligan.

"Sully, are you there?"

"Huh," was his only response as he lay still. A head injury, it was hard to tell how serious.

"Sully, stay with me," Anya said as she looked over Sulligan's head and shoulder. He had crumpled in a fairly straight line, head to toe, and Anya didn't see any serious bleeding.

Anya's brain was on serious overload now; first the feeling of dread, of Gustof in trouble, and now Sulligan was seriously hurt. She got a pillow from a cabinet and she slid the pillow under Sulligan's head.

"What… What happened?" Sulligan was awakening from his collapse but was very groggy.

"Don't try to speak right now," Anya said quietly to Sulligan as she leaned over him, still inspecting him for injuries. "Just lay there for now. Can you move your fingers and toes?"

In response Sulligan grabbed Anya's fingers in his hand.

"Are we in danger…the aliens, did they follow us?"

"No Sully, we're safe." She held his fingers in her hand. "Don't speak, just rest right now."

"The ship!"

"It's on automatic until we reach Earth."

Sulligan tried to stand. He made it half-way up and then collapsed again to the floor.

"Anya, I heard you say something is wrong," Sulligan stammered.

"Not the ship, its Gustof."

~ ~ ~ ~ ~

Gustof was sitting across the large walnut desk from the Explorers Guild's head of security. The two men stared at each other for several minutes. The Security Chief, Commander Skarieber looked over at Gustof, wondering to himself how this man was the target of such a security threat to the Guild.

The security branch, with Ashe leading the investigation, had uncovered a lot. They knew the who of the security breach, however, they were still trying to uncover the why and who any accomplices were. This couldn't have come at a worse time, what with the First Landing mission of Anya, Gustof's wife, and what she had discovered. It had to be quickly and quietly settled and Gustof kept safe.

Finally Commander Skarieber spoke.

"Gustof, how well do you know a fellow researcher, a Mr. Rayford. Apparently you went to school with him."

"Rayford, I don't remember a Rayford. May I have a mug of coffee?"

"Certainly Mr. Tyszko." The commander spoke into a monitor at his desk. "Two mugs of coffee."

The Commander looked at Gustof again before speaking.

"Are you sure? This Stefen Rayford seems to know you very well."

"Stefen, you mean my old college buddy. Yeah, I just didn't remember his last name was Rayford."

"Yes, not a surprise about that, he changed his last name about six years ago to his mother's maiden name. It was Stefen Wallace."

Gustof nodded up and down as he spoke.

"Yeah, Stefen, he was just at the farm. He said he was in the area doing inspections for the Guild and looked me up."

"Gustof," the Commander began as he got up from his seat and walked to the office window, looking out at the park laid out before him. "Gustof, Stefen was the saboteur. And worse, he left the Guild just before he changed his name."

The Commander walked back to his desk and sat down. The coffee arrived, brought to them by the Commander's orderly.

"Why me?" Gustof asked aloud.

"That's what we are trying to find out. Somehow he got into the high security research center in Greenland and stole the spores. He had to have had help. That's why you're here. For your protection and to help discover who else is behind this."

"OK, but how can I help?"

"Stefen has vanished. That is very hard to do these days. If you can think of anything that can help us find him, tell Ashe. It's disturbing, we have so many open questions in this investigation. And your wife, Anya, is do back soon."

"She found something, something big, didn't she," Gustof stated clearly.

"Yes, I can't tell you more. I read the files on the two of you. You have some sort of connection," the Commander said.

Before Gustof could answer, Commander Skarieber rose from his seat and walked to the door, opening it.

"That will be all for now, Gustof. If you think of anything, anything at all that, might help us, tell Ashe immediately. No matter how small a detail."

"Yes…" Gustof stammered as he left the room and joined the waiting Ashe.

~ ~ ~ ~ ~

After waiting an hour for Sulligan to recover a little bit laying on the floor, Anya helped the still very unsteady Sulligan to his feet and walked him to his berth she had folded out from the wall in the long range craft's sleeping area.

"You need rest, Sully, that is a serious head injury."

Sulligan tried to sit up on the edge of his berth, only to lay back down on his back, grabbing his right shoulder.

"That may be broken, Sully."

"What happened?" Sulligan asked his Senior Explorer.

"Don't you remember?" Anya asked, now even more concerned.

"No, I just remember waking up on the floor," Sulligan answered her.

"Sully, I'll get you something for the pain. You have a head injury as well as your shoulder. I don't know how serious it is, but it's not good."

"The ship…," Sulligan tried to ask.

"The ship is fine, Sully."

"The aliens, did they follow us?"

"No Sully, there is no sign of them."

Anya looked at Sulligan on his sleeping berth as she stood over him. He was in pain and maybe a little delirious. Then she thought once more of Gustof. Something was wrong on Earth and she knew it.

Three more weeks until home; Anya felt helpless. Sulligan's injuries could be beyond her medical abilities and what about Gustof, she could do nothing for him so far from Earth.

She composed a brief message to the Guild Headquarters.

—Sulligan hurt.
Unsure the severity.
How is Gustof?
Is he safe? —

~ ~ ~ ~ ~

The search for Stefen Rayford had begun within a few weeks of the discovery of the spore in Gustof's greenhouse. Ashe was personally leading the effort by the Guild's security unit, reporting directly to Commander Skarieber. Right away in the investigation Stefen's name rose to the top of the suspect list from Gustof's logbook. And then Ashe had found a retina scan of his in the Greenland base's security log. A retina scan that didn't match the name attached to it in the research centers database.

Stefen Rayford, or Stefen Wallace, wasn't showing up in any AI searches anywhere on Earth. Could he have gone off-planet? Ashe didn't think so. That just didn't meet the profile. He had targeted Gustof alone they now knew. And he would stick around until the job was done.

Stefen had changed his identity once; it was hard but not impossible, especially with so many living off-world. He would take the identity of the colonist, that made sense, however there were now millions who had gone off-world. And a small percentage of those who left would return to Earth, unable to succeed in an off-world environment with all of its challenges.

That would be the starting point. The Guild kept a database of the returning colonist. They regularly did research on why they returned so that they could better assist the next batch of colonist. Somebody Gustof knew. It was a starting point. Ashe would talk to

Gustof the next day to try to narrow the search parameters. Stefen was out there and she'd find him.

Early the next morning Ashe paid Gustof a visit in his apartment in the complex. Gustof was surprised but not unhappy to see her. It was almost too quiet in the complex and he had little to keep himself occupied with. He had reread the Agg journals that were available to him several times now.

"Any new leads on Stefen," he asked her as he welcomed her into the spacious apartment the Guild had given him to live in during the ordeal. Gustof was preparing his breakfast and a mug of Anya's coffee the Guild had supplied him with. The coffee helped keep him grounded in this crisis and near to Anya.

"He's somewhere, Gustof, I'll find him. That's why I am here."

"How can I help," Gustof replied. "Do you want some coffee?"

They walked to the main room of the apartment and Ashe took a seat while Gustof got her a mug of the coffee.

"Do you want any breakfast, Ashe?" Gustof said from the small kitchen. "I made sausage and eggs."

"No thanks, Gustof. I'll take the coffee; get my brain working with it. But I already had my breakfast. You go ahead and eat yours, though."

Gustof walked back out of the kitchen, Ashes mug of coffee in one hand, his plate of breakfast food in the other with his own mug of coffee balancing on it. Gustof sat down, putting the mugs and his plate on the small table. He took a drink of his coffee and waited for Ashe to pick-up her mug or start talking.

After a few minutes of waiting Gustof started the conversation between bites of food.

"OK, Ashe, how can I help?"

Ashe paused a moment from drinking her mug of coffee and smiled. "This is so good, Gustof. Not like what I usually drink here. Where did you get it from?"

Gustof frowned. He wanted answers; however he was starting to realize that the people of the Security Office always started with something not related to the investigation. Part of their training and now ingrained into the dna.

"The Guild was able to get it for me. It's from an island off the mouth of the Congo River."

Gustof looked directly at Ashe.

"Why are you here and how can I help?" Gustof bluntly asked her.

Ashe sat back in the chair and put down her mug of coffee. She looked straight at Gustof and spoke, slowly and clearly.

"I think he changed his name, his identity again."

"Ok," was Gustof quick response.

"I think that he wants to stay close to you, to finish the job. The Commander thinks the same. That's why you're here, Gustof…" she paused. "I think that he has assumed the identity of a colonist, somebody you knew in the past."

"But that would be off-world," Gustof questioned.

"A lot of colonist return and that database is not as complete as we thought. I think its somebody that you went to school with."

"That's a lot of people," Gustof said with a trace of skepticism.

"I know. However we can limit it to biological males for starters. Did you have a lot of friends in school?"

"A few good ones, but most were just acquaintances like Stefen."

"I think that it's somebody that you both knew. I know that Michael knew him from school as well as you, any others?"

Gustof paused his eating and took a drink from his mug before putting it down. He leaned back in the sofa he was sitting on. Michael, Stefen; a connection from school, that was it.

Gustof had introduced the two at the University at the old College Inn Pub near the campus. He was still in touch periodically with a few others from that crowd, but they were Earth-bound like him.

"Did you think of something, Gustof," Ashe expectantly asked Gustof.

"Yeah, maybe, a place we'd all hangout. There was about a dozen of us in our regular crowd there. I introduced Stefen to the group there."

"Can you think of their names, anything," Ashe excitedly said, picking up her pad to write on. Could this be the lead that they were looking for.

Gustof put his hand to his chin, rubbing it. He was starting to grow some whiskers there since he had been brought to the security complex. He would have to shave those before Anya got home. Who else was there? A few women, not what they were looking for. Gustof started thinking back and then speaking aloud his thoughts.

"There was Gary French, he was like the leader, but he's Earth-bound," Gustof spoke.

"That's good, another lead we can follow up on besides Michael. I think that pub is where we'll find the answer," Ashe said, trying to encourage Gustof.

"Let's see, there was Paul Short, and he really was short and we called him Shorty," Gustof added to his list. "He lives in Paris now, I hear from him every once and a while."

"Go on," said Ashe, entering his information onto her pad.

"Lewis Greenpants and Eric Johnson, they both talked about joining a colony for their research. I haven't heard from either of them in years."

"Those are solid leads then. Did they all graduate about the same time as you?"

"Yes, a year or two either way."

"Any others… think hard…this is great."

"Yeah, one more, Masi Aramaki," Gustof added. "I'm not sure were he is, we lost touch years ago."

"This is great Gustof, I think we'll find Stefen off this list."

Ashe got up to leave. She turned back to Gustof as she left.

"I'm going to follow up with the Commander on this. We'll reach out to Michael and Gary for any other names as well."

~ ~ ~ ~ ~

Anya was sitting in her command seat, her mind in turmoil. Sulligan was still laying on his sleeping berth behind the ships command station. He was still incoherent at times and it had already been several days. His shoulder seemed to be OK, no break as she had feared, but the concussion was a serious one. She had received a message from the Guild's medical corp.

—Medical attention will be waiting for Sulligan.

Gustof is looking forward to seeing you —

Gustof, was the other thing on her mind. They were so interconnected. She knew that he was in trouble; the message from the Guild didn't soothe that feeling. The Guild was saying nothing about whatever the issue was. Tears came briefly to her eyes.

"Mr. Branch, I'll be home soon," she said aloud to herself.

They were still about ten days from Earth's orbit. Ten days and she was on her own.

Anya got to her feet and walked back to where Sulligan was asleep in his berth. She took his hand in hers and held it briefly. The lump on his head was going down at least and the redness was going away. She had received limited instructions from the Guild concerning Sulligan. It was OK for her to give him limited doses of the painkiller they had onboard and she periodically checked his pulse for any irregularities. The Guild medical stressed that it was important for her to keep him lying in bed with his feet elevated. She put circulation socks on him from their medical supplies as per their instructions. If Sulligan was to get up for any reason, such as using the toilet facility, she was to guide him. Conversation with him was a good thing as it would help with the diagnosis by what he remembered or fixated on.

"Anya, are we home," Sulligan softly said as he opened his eyes and he briefly woke up.

"Not yet, but we are getting close. You just rest. I'll get you up when its time to land."

Anya stood and let go of Sulligan's hand.

"OK," he said as he fell back to sleep.

Chapter 11

"Mr. Tyszko, welcome to the heart of the Guild," the Guild Director stated as she shook Gustof's hand. "From here we track every mission that we are currently engaged in. Currently we have 14 ongoing missions, from ready to launch to the near-term return of your wife."

Mystified still why he was there, Gustof asked the Director point-blank. "And why am I here?"

"We'll get to that in detail shortly," she said, trying to maintain her even composure. In her mind her thoughts were racing. It was in her tenure that the two most significant finds of the Guild in its history were occurring right now through the work of the wife of the man standing before her. At the same time she had been told of the attacks aimed at Gustof Tyszko. A security guard from the Commanders office had accompanied Gustof to the Guild's Communication Center.

"Right now, Mr. Tyszko,..."

"Call me Gustof, please."

"Gustof, then, thank-you, right now we'd like you to record a brief message to Anya,. We'll send it out with our next batch of messages."

"When will she be back," Gustof asked.

"The end of next week," the director answered.

"That soon."

"Yes, they are well on their way back. We are within a few days of exchanging voice messages. We should have an answer back to the message we are sending in a few days. We'll call you back then."

"What do you want me to say?" Gustof asked the director.

The director paused before answering.

"We just want you to let her know that you are OK, just that. Don't mention Stefen or the investigation. We just want to reassure her about you."

"Why?" Is she OK?" Gustof answered back, now worried about his Senior Explorer. None of this was according to the protocol he knew.

"She's fine. However, Sulligan had a serious accident on the way back. She is trying to take care of him and is worried about you. Something in regard to the connection that you have."

"Is Sulligan OK?"

"He'll be fine once they land. He has a head injury that needs to be treated here at the Guild. Anya is doing what she can for him. We'll have doctors waiting for him when they land. That's why we need the message from you to her. Take some of the load she is carrying off of her."

The director escorted Gustof across the large room to another door. Here she handed Gustof over to another of the Guilds personnel, his bodyguard remaining alongside of him.

"Thank-you, Gustof. Enjoy our facilities. I'll call for you again when I get a reply."

As the Director turned to walk back to the Communications Center she said to Gustof. "She's doing wonderful, handling the mission and all. We'll tell you more next time."

Gustof now found himself outside the main building once more. A second security person now walked over to Gustof and joined the first in his protection detail. As Gustof looked back at the Guild's Communication Center, he thought of the Director's last words to him. They were more than a little confusing to him; if Anya was really OK, why all of the subterfuge? As he was thinking of Anya it seemed that he had reached her mind and he could feel the anxiety in it. She wasn't doing OK; he knew that.

~ ~ ~ ~ ~

Anya was just sitting in her command seat staring through the ships forward portal into space. Sulligan was right now lying on his berth. She had given him another dose of the mild sedative they carried on board the long-range ship. The Guild's medical didn't want him to receive too much of it. Like Anya they were worried about bleeding on his brain or brain swelling.

Her mind drifted to Gustof, she could feel him there with her. She could feel his worry for her and Sulligan. And there was something else in that connection she was feeling right then. She now positively knew that Gustof was in serious trouble. And why the Guild had him staying at its headquarters.

Gustof was still too far away to help. Sulligan, now badly injured, she was doing what little she could for him; that was her job right now, taking care of Sulligan.

She listened to the recording again of Gustof's message to her.

> —Doing great.
> Guild has me in a nice apartment.
> (She thought it strange he wasn't staying in hers.)
> Getting tours of the facility.
> Guild personnel always with me.
> (Always with him, why she thought.)
> Met the Director —

'That last part,' she thought. 'They were actually protecting him from something. She clinched her fist and pounded the consul. She wanted to scream. The only thing stopping her was Sulligan waking up.

She had to get control of herself. She pushed her seat back and remained there for several minutes, trying to calm down and not to think for a minute about everything going on around her. She closed her eyes, picturing the oak tree she and Gustof would sit underneath. That memory began to calm her down. She got up from her command seat to go back to the waking Sulligan and see how he was.

Seven days to home and Gustof.

~ ~ ~ ~ ~

Gustof had an early afternoon meeting with Ashe. She had mentioned on the video call that they had a new lead to find Stefen.

Gustof reached the security building, where Ashe was working, accompanied by his chaperones. After the usual security precautions, Gustof was let into a different wing of the security building than he had been in before.

"I thought I was meeting Ashe in her office," Gustof questioned the security guard leading him and his escort down the hallway. He was a little taken aback by the change in location. And he was a little worried; paranoia from the lingering effects of the spore or a real paranoia about Stefen. Gustof stopped for a second to get himself under control.

"Are you alright, sir? Ashe just thought that the large video viewing room would be easier than her office."

"I'm OK," Gustof said, taking deep breaths. "I'll be fine. Video room?"

"I don't have the details, sir, but she wanted to see you there. This way, just a couple of more doors down the hall."

They came to another secured door and Gustof's guide punched in his code to the door, No retina scan, those were just used to get into the Security Center and any high level offices. Ashe was waiting for Gustof inside and rose from her seat to greet him.

"Are you being treated OK, Gustof?"

"They're treating me great. Like a VIP. And I was just able to send a message to Anya."

"That's wonderful. Have a seat over here," Ashe said, motioning to a seat facing a blank wall. "We have made some real progress. Your friend in Paris, Paul Short, was a lot of help. I got the impression he never trusted Stefen."

Gustof walked over to the offered seat and sat down facing the wall. Ashe took the seat next to him.

"You went to Paris and saw Shorty?" Gustof asked Ashe.

"Yes, just a quick trip, but I think we found something. Like I said, he was a lot of help. Before I forget he said to say hello to you and that you owe him a visit."

Gustof and Anya had visited Shorty several times in Paris in the past.

Ashe now got serious. She spoke into a small hand-held mic and the wall in front of them changed into a large video screen.

"Gustof, I need you to focus on the video I'm going to play. It's from a colonist return station. The name and ID given was of your friend, Eric Johnson. See if you recognize him in any of the surveillance videos."

"OK, I'll give it a try. I'm surprised Eric would want to return from a colony. He was always so gung-ho about it."

"That's what Paul said and it gave us a solid lead. We tracked down Eric's ID to this return station. I'll begin the video now; tell me if you recognize anybody."

"OK."

The room darkened and the video feeds began. After each 10 videos Ashe asked Gustof if he recognized anybody. He almost did a couple of times, but it wasn't the person he thought when the video was replayed. Finally, after almost an hour of watching the videos and nothing, Gustof asked her to stop the videos for a break.

"Nothing, G," Ashe said, disappointed. "We have another hour of videos to watch."

"I'm good; my eyes just needed a break, and my brain. Can I have a coffee?"

"Coffee, sounds good. I'll get us each a mug. I'm afraid that it will just be the Guild's coffee roast."

"That's fine."

While Ashe left to get the coffee, Gustof sat back and closed his eyes. The people in the videos had started to run into each other in his mind. He started thinking of Anya. 'She'll be home in just 5 days,' he thought. Then he thought back to a memory of them together.

It was a few years earlier. They had gone to a jazz club while visiting St. Louis. He remembered them sitting at a small table near the stage, holding hands while they shared a warm brandy together. The daydream brought some clarity to his mind.

When Ashe came back into the video room she saw Gustof sitting straight up in his chair. As she handed Gustof his mug of coffee he looked up at her with a very direct look.

"Ashe, we need to replay a video from before, about 2 cycles back."

"Do you remember something?"

"I think so, I just missed it before."

"OK, we'll go back 2 videos."

Ashe spoke into the mic and a video began playing on the screen. Gustof took a big sip of his coffee as he now intently watched.

"Stop… go Back… a little further… stop!"

The video stopped where Gustof directed and he just stared at the screen for several minutes. Then he got up from his chair and walked up to the screen. He just stared at a figure in the background.

Gustof pointed at the screen and asked Ashe, "Can you make that image larger, that man in the back?" he said as he pointed at the figure on the screen. Ashe spoke into the mic again and the image was enlarged where Gustof had pointed. A tall man with a goatee, it was him, without a doubt, he had just seen Stefen a few weeks before.

"That's him, Stefen, the man in the back, there." He pointed.

Ashe got up and walked to the screen. She spoke into the mic as she stared at the man.

"Zac, can you mark that man in the video. Anymore shots of him?"

Ashe listened as Zac answered affirmatively.

"Gustof, we are going to play some video of the man that you pointed out. We have quite a few shots of him. Let me know, is that Stefen or Eric?"

The screen started showing a series of video shots of the figure in question. One showed him entering in the info of Eric at a security consul. There was no doubt in Gustof's mind.

"That is not Eric. That is Stefen. He was clean shaven when I last saw him, but that's him."

Ashe immediately got on the phone next to her chair with the Commander.

"We have him, Sir. It's like you thought, using one of Gustof's old friend's ID; Eric Johnson."

Ashe listened for a few minutes to the Commander and then looked over at Gustof, her face ashen.

"Are you sure, Sir?"

A few more minutes of silence from Ashe as she listened, and when she finished she looked over at Gustof again. Finally, she spoke.

"Gustof, I have some news. A bit of scary news, however we are covering it. Stefen is here at the Guild Headquarters plantation. The name Eric Johnson has appeared in several places with Stefen's picture."

"Here!"

"Yes. I am supposed to escort you right to the Commander's office. Armed security will join us."

"Armed security, not just my chaperones."

"Gustof, I want to be honest with you. What you and your friends discovered was just the tip of the iceberg. Stefen is now, it seems, part of a radical group... and he wants you dead."

Gustof started shaking on hearing those words.

There was a knock on the door and Ashe drew her weapon. She walked over to the door and used its intercom.

"Who is this, your password."

"This is your security detail. Pass code… Delilah."

"Are they alright?" A worried Gustof asked Ashe.

"Yes, they are the Commander's own security. The password he just now created when I was on the phone with him. Let's go, things are going to happen quickly now."

~ ~ ~ ~ ~

Anya and Sulligan were sitting at the long-range crafts table in the back of the ship. Sulligan's sleeping berth was back in place in the wall so they could sit at the table. A mug of coffee was in front of each of them; two more days of coffee was left. That was OK, Anya thought, they were only three days from Earths orbit.

Sulligan was starting to feel better, he was now able to walk OK and the coffee seemed to help him think. He was sitting up at the table, mug in hand, drinking his coffee and talking about a little bit of everything. Most of what he said was coherent and made sense. However, at times, what he said made no sense at all. He was aware that he was on the ship and remembered most of their landing. The aliens were his big concern. He seemed convinced that they had followed them.

One more day and earths tracking systems would pick them up and guide them the rest of the way home to their landing.

Sulligan wanted to get back to work studying the planets lost language. Over Anya's objections he had pulled up his work on the ship's computer. After just a few minutes he had had to stop; the pounding headaches returned.

"I don't remember, Anya. I know I had begun to make sense of the planets language, but now I just don't remember."

"This is going to take time, Sully, and you have a bad injury."

Sulligan just looked over at her. He knew that he was hurt, he just didn't know how badly. Neither of them did.

"Do you need me at the controls," Sulligan asked his Senior Explorer. He wanted to do something, anything, to help.

"Everything is on automatic now. Not too much to do."

"Cataloguing, research, I need to do something," Sulligan loudly voiced. "I feel helpless."

Anya looked over at him, wishing that she could offer more. She could see that Sulligan was close to losing it at times. She had added some more of the sedative to his coffee. That would help to keep him calm.

"Let's watch a video, Sully, there are still a few we haven't watched. Something light to help us rest."

"OK," Sulligan said, looking up from his coffee at her. "I think we have one more serving of popcorn left. Should I go get it?"

"That would be great, Sulligan. I'll load up an old musical, *Seven brides for seven brothers*, that should be fun."

Sulligan seemed to brighten up as he got up from the bench. It was only making the popcorn, but at least that was something he could do for them.

~ ~ ~ ~ ~

Stefen looked around nervously. None of this had gone as planned. He and the others, they thought it was all worked out. Gustof, he had no business winning that award. It should have gone to himself and his friends.

The switch in identity had worked at first; the idea of taking Eric's identity had been a stroke of genius. A few switched security scans and he had been able to go wherever he was needed for the small group's plans.

What had gone wrong?

Stefen looked at himself in the mirror. The goatee had to go, but what to do about it and his face; grow a full beard or shave it off. During his career with the Guild he had been clean shaven. He had only grown the goatee to look more like Eric. And now, somehow, that cover was blown. His contact with the group had briefly talked to him.

"Stay close and inside. They think they've found you."

A full beard it was, then, and he would dye it and his hair blond. He looked at his blue eyes, almost grey; green eyes it would be; colored contacts; that would help a lot. That with the blond hair and full beard should be enough. Stefen picked up a bottle of instant hair dye and worked it into his hair and beard. He would use some hair growth enhancer to fully grow out his beard.

Stefen was startled as he heard a soft knock at his door. He walked to the door past a small table where he picked up his fire-arm. They hadn't planned that it would go like this. It was just supposed to be a non-violent way to slow down the colonization he had been told. It was wrong, what the Guild was doing to the planets they found.

As Stefen stopped at the door without opening it, he thought back to how the group had found him. He had just lost the contract to Gustof. In his anger at the Guild he had lashed out at the Guild's decision makers. One had been hurt in the altercation, not badly, but it had been enough to have him suspended from the Guild.

The group had come to the pub, not far from the Guild's headquarters. Stefen had started drinking pretty heavily. Not much else to do since his suspension. He didn't know if he still had a career with the Guild or not.

They had planted the seed in Stefen's head; the sabotage of Gustof's work. That in turn sparked further outrage that Stefen had directed at Gustof. They would have to do it surreptitiously, being careful to avoid Guild security.

They arranged for Stefen to be permanently expelled from the Guild; in a quiet way so as to not disparage Stefen's reputation. His expulsion was covered up in the Guild's own security offices; they had somebody of their own in those offices. Now Stefen was forced to their cause, there could be no backing out for him. Stefen looked through the old keyhole in the door at the person on the other side. He had only met a few members of the cause; he was told there were not many. They had to be careful with who they recruited. At the door was the person who first made contact with him that first night at the pub. Stefen opened the door and let him in.

Stefen started talking at the man the moment he closed the door.

"How did they find me? I thought my identity was secure."

The man saw the firearm in Stefen's hand and waved for him to sit down. 'This isn't good,' the man was thinking. 'Stefen was always a wildcard in this.'

As the two men sat down, Stefen keeping his firearm in his hand, the visitor began to speak.

"We're not sure how they broke down the identity we gave you. Eric is still off-world on the *vacation* we arranged."

"You said we had somebody in the security office to cover this."

"We do," the visitor spoke. "Stop waving that gun around, Stefen, the last thing we need is for that to go off."

Stefen calmed down for a moment and set the gun down at his side, but still within reach.

"What about that security officer? Can I still get to Gustof? I want to finish this off, give him what he deserves."

The paranoia that had come to grip Gustof from the spore was now affecting Stefen. He had actually carried it in his pocket for quite a while, while Gustof had only come into casual contact with it in the greenhouse. The conspirators had made sure of that. All to better control Stefen.

"Right now he is secure in the Guild's Security Headquarters building. We can't touch him for the moment."

"But what about our inside man?" Stefen said, once more getting agitated and standing up, his fist clenched.

The visitor knew that he had to be careful with Stefen. That's why the group chose him for this. It wasn't quite time for the next step in the plan; taking the Explorer's Guild down a notch.

"Patience, Stefen, you are safe here. I see that you are changing your hair color, that's good. Any other changes? Right now our man can't get close to Gustof, so he's backing off. But when Anya returns…"

"Anya... what does she have to do with any of this? I thought it was about Gustof and his research."

The visitor stood up and handed Stefen the package he was carrying; it was a large envelope.

"Inside this is your new identity. Stay here until we call for you. We'll have your meals brought up to you."

"Then I'll get off-world, start over like you promised," Stefen said as he walked to the small kitchen and poured himself a drink.

"Yes, all of that. Right now this is a safe place for you. Lots of these vacant apartment's on the Guild's campus. This is the best place for you until it's time. This apartment is not in yours or Eric's name, just that of another off-worlder who had the sense to return and joined our cause."

Stefen glanced out of the window. Where ever he looked outside, the streets bustled with activity. And wherever he looked he saw security people looking for him, both real and imagined. They weren't even trying to hide from him.

"You'll know what to do when I return," the visitor said as he got up from his seat and walked to the door. He added as he left the apartment, "And where to go?"

"Yes," Stefen answered. "I know the campus very well."

"In two days then," the visitor finished as he turned and left.

~ ~ ~ ~ ~

They had finally reached Earth's orbit. They would be landing tomorrow at the Guild's landing pad not far from the campus. Anya was now in almost hourly communication with the Guild's medical personnel.

"Do I need to sedate him before we land?" Anya asked the doctors as Sulligan slept in his berth. She had started giving Sulligan stronger doses of the sedative now that she was in direct communication with the doctors.

"How is he behaving?" they asked her.

The headaches and nausea are getting worse, again. He's dizzy as he tries to stand. Now he's getting frustrated and belligerent. He knows something is wrong and he feels helpless.

"That is to be expected with his serious head injury. We'll be waiting for you with an ambulance as soon as you touch-down. You're doing a great job with this, Anya."

"Thank-you," Anya replied, looking back at the sleeping Sulligan.

She looked out the front portal of the ship; the Earths moon was coming into view. That made her think of Gustof once more, they used to sit under the oak tree and watch the moon together. Anya had told him about visiting the station on the moon and its small colony. He had just shaken his head when she suggested they visit it together.

"That would take the magic away from looking up at it," he had told her. Now she thought she understood what he meant. There was a magic in looking at the moon, from Earth or from space.

Gustof needed her help, now more than ever. She was determined about getting to him. The doctors were there to take care of Sulligan; she needed to be there to take care of Gustof and give him her strength.

Anya was broken out of her thoughts by Sulligan waking up. She watched from her command chair as Sulligan tried to stand. Then she remembered his injuries.

"Wait until I get there, Sully. Let's have our last mug of coffee. Just sit there until I bring it to you."

Sulligan sat back down on the edge of his berth.

"OK, I'll wait," he slightly slurred. "We can fold up my berth and sit at the table to plan our landing."

"That sounds like a good idea, Sully," Anya answered as she looked with concern at Sully. She was surprised the doctors gave her permission to give him the coffee once she conferred with them.

"Just a little, with the sedative," they had told her.

She could now visibly see the slight swelling just above his right temple on the side of his head. As the last of their coffee was brewing, Anya walked back to her command seat and picked up the bottle of the sedative. There wasn't much left.

When it was time for the actual landing procedure's to begin she'd walk Sulligan up front to his command chair and get him strapped in. Once secure she'd give him the last of the sedative with the syringe.

The landing itself would have to be done on automatic with the Guild's computer guiding the ship in. That would normally be the combined job of the Senior Explorer and their apprentice. However, she would still be in her own command seat, ready to switch the controls to manual, just in case.

~ ~ ~ ~ ~

Gustof lay back on his bed in the Guild's Security offices apartments. Two armed guards were stationed outside the door and two were inside the apartment with him. The Guild was taking no chances with his security. Each of them was from the Commanders own security detail. He had gotten to know the security personnel, his chaperones, pretty well. They took their job seriously and Gustof had come to like the ones assigned to his protection. While not friends per se, he had found a lot to talk about with them. Anya would be landing tomorrow. The commander had told him that they were waving some of the isolation security protocols because of the security threat. Sulligan would be taken directly to the Guild's hospital and Anya would be brought directly to the security offices under heavy guard. She would debrief there and spend her isolation with Gustof in the apartment.

Chapter 12

They finished their second orbit around the earth, slowing down in the process, and began the long glide path to the Guild's landing area. The Guild's navigation computer was in control of the craft now.

Anya sat at her command station, both Sulligan and her strapped in. Sulligan was pretty much out of it with the last dose of the sedative Anya had given him. Anya watched him closely, concerned as he passed in and out of consciousness.

They penetrated the upper atmosphere of the Earth and the ship was a little bit off-balance. Not much, but Anya kept her eyes on the controls, ready to take over if necessary. The long-range craft extended it stubby delta wings and the Guild's computer kept the craft on course.

Anya glanced at the video screen showing a rear view and each of the delta wings were extended out. Wings fully deployed now, Anya was a little concerned about the winglet on the starboard side. While the winglet on the port side seemed ready to extend out and up once they reached 20,000 feet, the starboard one seemed *off*. She wasn't sure what she saw but it concerned her.

They were approaching the 20,000 feet of elevation mark, when the winglets would extend out for better control of the craft and the portside wingtip extended up and out in one graceful move. Anya watched the starboard one; it slid out only partially and seemed to stop, partially deployed. She could feel the craft *slip* as the uneven wings forced the craft off the center line.

"Guild control, I have a situation here," was Anya's calm call to the Guild's Control Center (GCC).

"Control here, what is your situation?"

"Starboard winglet failed to deploy fully."

"We'll relaunch its command from here. Let us know the result."

"Still over 2400 miles to go," Anya answered as she observed the malfunctioning winglet. "Plenty of time to get it right."

Anya waited as the command was resent from the Guild Control computer; no change in the winglet.

"GCC, no change in the winglet, what do you recommend?"

"You are too far in to redeploy your craft and try again."

"I am aware of that GCC," a now worried Anya stated. "What do you recommend?"

"Are you still on your own at the controls," GCC asked Anya, aware of Sulligan's injuries.

"Yes, Sulligan is unavailable to help."

"Watch your center line, we'll try to keep the craft level from here. 10,000 feet altitude is the critical point. That's still three hours away."

Anya anxiously watched the altimeter as the craft descended over the Pacific ocean. The landing port was on the coast to allow these long glide paths; approaching 15,000 feet, then almost 12,000 feet. Anya received a message from the GCC.

"We are having trouble keeping you trim right now. At 10,000 feet we suggest you move to manual control. Can you handle that?"

"Yes, GCC, manual control at 10,000 feet." Anya had been getting ready for that since it was clear the one winglet would not fully deploy.

"That will put you an hour out and the ride will get bumpy for you. Weather is clear, all the way in. Maximum wind speed less than 10 knots. Just keep that one wing up."

As Anya approached 10,000 feet in the craft she took a last look at Sulligan safely strapped in. The landing was going to be tough with just her at the controls. Training for this was based on the both of them controlling the flight path together. Somehow, she felt Gustof inside of her. "You can do this Mrs. Branch, you can do this."

10,000 feet and she switched the controls to manual. She felt the GCC computer switch off and the craft tried to dip to the starboard side. She hit the manual control to extend the wingtip one more time; nothing. One more glance at Sulligan, then all of her focus was on the controls in front of her. It was taking both hands and all of her strength to keep the wheel steady and the wings level. 'I'm coming Mr. Branch,' she thought to herself, somehow gaining more strength.

5,000 feet and the wings were still somehow staying level; it was like she had a co-pilot alongside her, helping her. "You can make it, Mrs. Branch, I'm right here." She could swear she heard Gustof's words right there with her.

2,500 feet and she lowered the wheels; twenty wheels deploying and snapping into place. She almost felt that as much as she saw the board light up from it.

500 feet from the ground now. She glanced at her air speed; 250 knots, almost perfect; seconds now until landing. She held the wheel tightly now, with both hands, as the wings kept wanting to dip down on the right side.

100 feet. Then touchdown, the wheels slightly bouncing before becoming steady on the landing pad. It would take a few miles to bring the ship to a stop, but at least she didn't have to worry about the wings now. Once the ship slowed to 100 knots she deployed the breaks; another mile and they came to a stop.

They were back.

"Thank-you, Mr. Branch, I'm home," Anya said aloud.

"I'm right here with you, Mrs. Branch," was the voice of Gustof she knew she heard right alongside her.

~ ~ ~ ~ ~

It was early afternoon and Gustof was standing in front of a large window watching Anya's craft come in for its landing. He could feel the anxiety that she was feeling at the controls of the craft. He knew that she had it under control. 'You can do this Mrs. Branch,' he was thinking. The wheels touched down; she was home.

Ashe joined Gustof in the community room. He was still standing by the window where he watched Anya land.

"How are you doing, Gustof. I bet you are relieved Anya is home."

Gustof turned around and met her half-way across the room. The smile on his face told her everything.

"You would win that bet," Gustof joked with her.

Ashe walked over to a table and sat down. They were alone in the room; the Guild had reserved it for Gustof so that he could watch the landing without any fear. Ashe motioned for Gustof to join her. When he sat down he could see the concern on her face.

'What is it, Ashe?"

"Gustof, don't get too alarmed, we have the situation under control."

Alarmed at the words Gustof started to stand up.

"Its under control, Gustof, please, sit down. Nothing is going to happen to you or Anya."

"Anya's a target now!" Gustof almost shouted, hesitating before retaking his seat.

"Yes, but we have found out a lot from the man we caught."

"So what is the story, now?" a fidgety Gustof asked.

"It's a small group that wants to end space travel as we know it. We now know that Stefen was recruited by them shortly after his employment with the Guild was terminated."

"So, how does Anya fit into their plans?"

"Somehow, word leaked out about what she found. They must have people inside the Guild itself."

"Was it that big?" Gustof asked. He knew that she had discovered something phenomenal, but he still had no idea what it was.

"Yes it was, Gustof. You're the first one outside of official Guild offices to find out, excepting the leak." Ashe paused for a second before speaking again. "We are going to make the news public shortly after Anya reports in. We had hoped to keep it contained, but now that its out, we'll do the announcement with Anya."

"So what is this big news?" Gustof asked again, feeling now Ashes excitement.

"Gustof, we are not alone in the universe."

"What, she met an alien?"

"Not met, but she saw their ship circling her First Landing world. I think that you can understand the importance of this."

Gustof just sat back in his chair, almost tipping back in it before he caught himself. Anya, his Anya; her dream and that of every First Landing explorer; first contact with an alien race. She had found proof that the Earth is not alone in the universe.

"Are they friendly?" Gustof finally asked Ashe.

"Too be honest, Gustof, we have no idea."

Gustof leaned forward, his elbows on the table, stunned.

"My Anya, first contact with another planet."

"Gustof, I know that this is a lot to take in. However, we still have the other matter to concern us with right now; Stefen and his anarchist friends. The commander asked me to bring you directly to his office once Anya had landed."

"What about Anya?"

"A special security detail will meet her and Sulligan at the landing site. You know Sulligan is injured."

"Yes, I know. How is he?"

"It's serious, but he'll be going directly to the medical center for triage and if necessary, surgery. Both he and Anya will be transported in armored vehicles."

"It's that serious now," Gustof softly said, the excitement of Anya's landing and discovery fading behind the urgency of the threat to them both.

"We think so," Ashe firmly answered. "Stefen is the key and we don't know where he is, other than he is close by. We are searching for him, but we just don't know."

"Let's go then. I guess my reunion with Anya will be in his offices."

"Yes, she will be escorted directly there."

As Ashe opened the door, four heavily armed security agents stood waiting for them. One of them held out a flak jacket for Gustof to put on and he helped Gustof into it.

"Is this necessary?" Gustof asked the man.

"Yes, sir, we know that Stefen is armed."

~ ~ ~ ~ ~

Stefen, now blond with a full beard, sat on a bench near the entrance of the security offices. The park he was in was made up of broad paths and manicured trees and lawn. There were hundreds of these benches around the park and people congregated around them in small groups.

Stefen was wearing the latest in unisex clothing, complete with earrings and a silver necklace. He looked nothing like he did during his time with the Guild. He had a new ID as well that they had given him; now he was Jules Papi, a free spirited poet and songwriter. They even had given him some of Jules books to hand out, something that one of the conspiracy members had written to give him more credibility.

Just wait, they had told him, he would know when to act.

~ ~ ~ ~ ~

The long-range craft had come to a stop on the runway and Anya began the shutdown procedures. That would normally be Sulligan's job, but he remained pretty out of it.

"Command Center, we are landed and preparing to exit the craft." A pretty routine announcement Anya thought.

"We have you on the board. Escort vehicles will arrive at your location shortly. Remain inside with the doors closed."

Anya didn't think anything of that. There was always the risk of contamination and she finished up the shutdown procedures. She figured that their craft would be towed to another location for decontamination and to be emptied.

About an hour later 3 vehicles arrived at the landing area and now Anya was alarmed when she saw them. Each of them was a heavily armored security vehicle. She knew that there was a security issue with Gustof but she hadn't expected this.

The three vehicles pulled up alongside the long-range craft's exit door and armed security personnel climbed out of them and fanned out around the craft. Anya heard a call on the communication consul.

"Anya, this is Command Central. Remain in your craft until security personnel have secured the area and wave you out."

Now this was alarming and unusual. Usually a returning craft was just towed to the decontamination area and that was it; protocol. This was definitely not protocol. 'Could it be her discovery,' Anya thought. 'Were they afraid that she would say something that wasn't dictated by the Guild?' At least she saw that one of the armored vehicles was an ambulance for Sully.

Once the security forces had fanned out into a rough circle around the long-range craft, Anya saw one of the personnel wave her out. A stretcher was being brought to the shuttle for Sulligan and the exit ramp was rapidly rolled into position at the exit door. Two of the security detail walked up the ramp to greet her. One carried a flak jacket to her. Behind them were two more security people with the gurney for Sulligan.

"What's this?" an alarmed Anya spoke loudly to the security team. "Am I under arrest?"

"No mam," the security guard with the flak jacket said. "This is for your protection."

"My protection from what?"

"There are armed threats against you, that's all I know. Please put on this flak jacket for your protection."

Anya reluctantly put on the offered flak jacket. Then she walked down the ramp, escorted on both sides by the security.

"What about Sulligan?" Anya said as she briefly stood her ground at the bottom of the ramp.

"He is being taken directly to the Guild's Medical Center, mam. He will be treated there, the lead security agent said calmly to her. "Please get into the carrier. We are exposed out here."

"What about my quarantine?"

"You will do that at the security center, as will each of us. We'll all be in quarantine together," he said as he softly took her arm to guide her to the carrier.

"Take me to Gustof, I have to see him," she almost shouted, getting agitated at all the security. This had to be about Gustof she now realized. All her thoughts of Sulligan's injuries now disappeared. Now she feared for Gustof more than anything else. 'What had happened to him?' she thought anxiously to herself. She could feel Gustof's anxiety levels from where she stood. She watched as Sulligan was quickly loaded into the ambulance and driven away.

"Our records and samples?" Anya asked the security detail as she loaded herself into the carrier.

"Everything is safe. Please seat yourself so that we can get underway," the lead agent said as he climbed in behind her. "Gustof will be waiting for you in the security center."

"The security center," she said as she seated herself.

The lead security agent secured the door behind him, walked bent over to the front of the passenger compartment and tapped on the window to the driver. "Let's move out."

Inside the cramped carrier Anya tried to question the security personnel in it with her.

"What's going on?" she pleaded.

The lead security guard sat down beside her.

"It's dangerous for you right now. Word leaked out of what you found. Your husband is waiting for you."

"Where are you taking me," Anya demanded, the continuous stress of Sulligan's injury, her concern for Gustof and the landing was starting to break her down. She started crying. "Take me to Gustof."

"That's what we're doing, mam. Your husband is safe and with the Security Commander."

"OK," she said as she slowly quieted down.

The armored vehicles drove away together. At the edge of the landing zone they were met by others. Two of them joined the ambulance as it sped away to the Guild's Medical Center. Three more joined the ones escorting Anya on the way to the Guild's Security Center and her reunion with Gustof.

~ ~ ~ ~ ~

It was mid-afternoon when Anya was escorted by the security personnel into the Commanders office. He was sitting behind his desk with Ashe standing to one side. Gustof was pacing nervously waiting for Anya; from the window to the door and back. The commander himself was going back and forth with his own eyes between Gustof and Ashe. They could both see the worry in his eyes.

Stefen had vanished. The security patrols could find no sign of him; however they knew he was close by. Word had leaked out prematurely of other life in the universe, life that was also exploring the cosmos. And that made the group behind Stefen even more dangerous.

A buzzer sounded on the Commander's desk. When he answered word came. Anya had arrived and entered the security complex and was entering the office building. She would be at his office in just a few minutes. The Commander looked up at Gustof and Ashe and finally smiled.

"She's in the building."

On hearing that Gustof stopped his pacing and just stood there. His Senior Explorer, Anya, was safe.

~ ~ ~ ~ ~

The Cabal was getting more desperate by the day in its efforts to stop altogether the colonization of space. They were never a large group, although they did have members inside the Explorer's Guild Control Center. That's how they had found out about Anya's discovery that other life was out there. Maybe now, in the eyes of the Cabal, they would get somewhere in slowing down the colonization efforts. And maybe now, slowing down the colonization wasn't enough. They quickly tried to spread rumors that the aliens were hostile; only to be laughed down by all.

The group now knew that one of its key members, the man who had recruited a disgruntled Stefen several years earlier, had been caught. Robert was a liability now; just how much would he divulge.

They were in a group, together now, almost twenty in number, each with their own instruments, singing folk songs from the distant past. They all could easily see Stefen close by, unrecognizable to the Guild's security, sitting on a bench alone, trying to hand out *his* books of poetry. Everything was set in place. It was almost time.

~ ~ ~ ~ ~

The captured member of the Cabal was in the Explorer's Guild's Security Offices, in a small interrogation room. The room was scarcely used since it was put in place next to the Commander's office. A video feed led to the wall video screen in his office. The Commander could use the video feed to watch a prisoner as they were being interrogated. Until now it had only been used twice in 25 years. Now the commander watched as the captured Cabal member sat behind a table being questioned by two security personnel.

They had picked him up off a random video feed when they thought they had Stefen cornered. The Cabal member, Robert, had just had a meeting with Stefen, however, by the time they had arrived at the apartment Stefen had once again gone into hiding. Robert, though, they were able to follow and they picked him up at his own apartment. That was just early this morning and he was brought to the Security Center almost immediately. Here his questioning was begun. So far Robert had remained silent. Per the Guild rules, drugs were not allowed in the questioning unless the suspect agreed.

"Where is Stefen?" they kept asking him.

"You'll never find him or any of us."

"What are your plans?"

"It's too late for any of you."

"We caught you, we'll catch the others."

"It doesn't matter, we're prepared."

Finally, after over two hours of this, the questionnaires just looked back at their Commander through the video feed as if to ask, what next?

The Commander just shook his head. Gustof was watching the screen as well. He rushed over to the panel, screaming.

"Why do you want to hurt Anya?"

Robert got up from his seat and calmly walked to the mirror. He knew that they could see him, even if he couldn't see them. He heard what Gustof had shouted at him through the system.

"We are not alone. Your Anya showed us that. She and the Guild must be stopped."

As the two security personnel dragged Stefen back to his seat he screamed at everybody.

"We are not alone!"

Gustof just stood there in shock. Anya would soon be in the office. He needed her and he knew that she needed him right now.

Commander Skarieber looked at Gustof and motioned for him to sit down. Ashe once more guided Gustof to his seat.

"Why Anya, why her?" Gustof quietly said as he sat down.

Gustof never took his eyes off the video feed as he sat there staring at Robert, who just sat there, quietly staring back.

Anya arrived in the Commander's office after a brief one-hour decontamination shower in the Security Offices. They had drawn her blood there and waited for the results before they brought her to the office where she would finish her report. Finally the all-clear was given, nothing unusual in her blood, and now dressed in a onesie, Anya was escorted by her assigned security to the Commander's office.

As Anya entered the office the security personnel with her stopped outside and joined the other security on-duty outside the Commander's office.

Nothing could hold Gustof back from rushing to her as she entered the room, not even the glare of the stubbornly non-compliant Robert on the screen. Their tight embrace seemed to last an eternity to the two of them, tears came from Gustof's eyes, he was so happy and relieved that Anya was home. Tears came to Anya's eyes as well as she kissed him; it was as if the two of them were alone in the room. The Commander and Ashe just watched in wonder at the magic of their love. The Commander had heard stories from Ashe and others about how their love seemed to cross the cosmos, and now he was seeing it first hand.

As Gustof and Anya calmed down in their embrace in each others arms, Ashe finally interceded. She touched each of them on their arms, almost gently, and spoke to them.

"If you could both sit down over here," she motioned at two chairs facing the video screen and Robert, "we have a lot to do to uncover that's going on."

After the two of them sat down, the Commander spoke.

"Anya, it's a pleasure to have the two of you here with me. I just wish it was under better circumstances. What you have discovered will change things forever, throughout Earth and its colonies."

"Thank you," Anya said, swiveling her chair to face the Commanders desk. Gustof did the same. "But why all of the security, I only got bits of it from Gustof."

Gustof just looked on, almost staring at Robert on the video screen.

"Who is that?" Anya finally broke the silence, asking the Commander directly, pointing at the man in the screen.

"That is Robert. He cannot see or hear us in this room, unless I let him. We can see and hear him. He is part of an anti-colonization, anti-space terrorist Cabal. We have been aware of them for some time. We never considered them especially dangerous until your husband's incident with Stefen Rayford," the Commander began before Anya interrupted him.

"Incident... Stefen... wasn't he at our wedding?" Anya rapid fired at the other three in the room.

Gustof took Anya's hand and began.

"Stefen is an old college acquaintance of mine and yes, he was at our wedding. He showed up at our farm shortly after you began your voyage. I thought it was just to get reacquainted. I hadn't realized he had been removed from the Guild. He told me he was traveling through the area on Guild's business. He planted a poisonous fungi spore into the greenhouse..."

Anya looked at Gustof, shocked by the revelation and interrupted again.

"I knew something was wrong, but poisonous fungi in the greenhouse."

Ashe took over the story now. "Anya, you should be glad that you and Gustof have such wonderful friends. It was they who uncovered the plot."

"Plot," Anya incredulously said. She was getting more anxious by the moment as she and Gustof squeezed each others hands.

"Yes, a plot, Anya," Gustof quietly said to her. "To sabotage my research."

"But... But... I don't know how to believe all of this." She looked at Gustof, "I knew something was wrong."

Ashe continued now.

"Your husband's friends found the spores by accident and Michael, whom I've known for years, identified the spore, its danger and contacted me."

The commander now spoke again.

"We eventually traced the spore, first through Stefen and Greenland and then through him to the Cabal. We arrested his accomplice in Greenland but that has gotten us no-where. We know now how dangerous the Cabal has become and Stefen, we think he is the key to finding them. We thought we had him trapped in an apartment here. Somehow he slipped away again and then we lost him."

"Lost him? Again? And Robert?" Anya fired the rapid questions again.

"We are pretty sure that Robert was Stefen's contact with the Cabal. We hope to get some clue as to Stefen's whereabouts and new identity from him. We just caught him this morning, so far nothing."

Gustof and Anya just looked at each other. Then they smiled and turned back to the Commander. "We'll find him," Gustof said with a renewed confidence with Anya there next to him. "Can we talk to him, and let him see us."

"Yes, of course," the Commander said. "We know that they have something big planned. Any help would be appreciated."

The commander spoke into the mic next to him.

"Open up the two-way vision and communication."

Anya and Gustof now spoke rapidly back and forth almost as one.

"Where would he hide?"

"Close by, in plain sight."

"He would have to look different."

"He always looked very professional; clean shaven, immaculately dressed."

"He would change that 100%"

"Would he be alone or with the others?"

"Alone, blending in, the others close by."

"Where is he, is he in the park?" Anya bluntly asked Robert, watching his body closely as he answered her.

Robert just looked back at them, silent, but his body twitched ever so slightly.

"He's in the park," Anya quickly stated.

They could see Robert squirm as she said that.

"Can we see video of the park, close by the entrance to the building?" Gustof asked the Commander.

"Yes of course,' Commander Skarieber said.

Half of the wall changed. They could still see Robert in the interrogation room, but half the wall turned into smaller video screens. Anya and Gustof walked up to the screens and started watching them and Robert. Their rapid back and forth started once more.

"The centennial park," they both saw and said as one. Anya saw Roberts eyes briefly change when they said it.

"He's in the park."

Anya took a long look at Robert now. She knew him from someplace. She had eaten lunch in the park a lot. That was it.

"I know him," Anya said, pointing at Robert. "I am trying to remember where I know him from."

Robert started squirming in his seat once more as he heard that. They could all see he was getting nervous.

"Think," the Commander said. "This could be the key we have been waiting for. Where do you know him from?"

"Just a second, "Anya said a she walked up to the screen showing Robert, back to the screens showing the park and then back to looking intently at Robert. "The park... he's a musician that plays with other musicians at the park, not far from the main entrance. They are there a lot."

Gustof watched Robert as Anya Stated that she had seen Robert with other musicians in the park. He could tell in an instant that was where they were; a group of musicians playing together in the park.

Gustof now spoke.

"He would be blonde now, not dark-haired like before, and a full, bushy beard so that we couldn't see his face."

It was Anya's turn now.

"He would dress completely different, the latest unisex clothing."

"And flamboyant!" Gustof added. He looked over at Robert. They had him.

"He would have on lots of jewelry. Would he have an instrument?"

"I don't think so," Gustof said. "He was pretty tone def and never could play anything."

"But he'd be near the musicians."

"Yes."

The Commander and Ashe just watched in wonder at the interplay banter between the two."

Finally, once Gustof and Anya took a brief breath, the Commander gave the command to the entirety of the security personnel.

"We have him, a description of Stefen." Robert just looked on in agony, confirming their suppositions. "Look for a tall man, blonde, with a full beard, sitting alone, with musicians nearby; unisex clothing and lots of jewelry. If spotted do not approach, notify me directly."

~ ~ ~ ~ ~

Stefen was sitting alone on a bench in the park near the security offices entrance. Musicians were playing near-bye. He was trying to hand out his poetry books as instructed by his handler when one of the musicians strode over. He, like Stefen, was wearing unisex clothing with lots of jewelry; in this case that included a kilt with an elaborate belt. The Cabal had seen how nervous Stefen looked and had sent the man over to calm Stefen down.

"Stay with us. You are one of us, now," the guitar player said. He strummed a couple of notes on his guitar as he sat down on the bench next to Stefen. The music was a signal for the others to join them.

The other musicians, in ones and twos, gradually made their way over to where Stefen sat. One of those who arrived handed Stefen a set of bongo's to play.

"Just pound them," he said. "Be one with us."

"Join in with us, you have no reason to fear," said another.

"They caught Robert, but it's too late to stop us," a woman playing a wooden flute softly spoke to the group.

"Robert?" Stefen asked, now more afraid.

"Your recruiter," another spoke. "But you are one with us."

On hearing that Robert, his recruiter to the Cabal, had been captured, Stefen truly began to panic as the paranoia began to settle in. He had been on the run for weeks now and they had already almost caught him several times. And now they had caught his handler.

"Calm yourself, brother, join us in our music. We have much to celebrate."

Stefen looked around himself, alarmed. He began to pull the gun out from beneath his tunic.

"Not now," the guitar player said as he forced Stefen's hands onto the bongos. "Just bang away, it's not time yet."

The musicians all were now gathered around Stefen, encircling him. They saw that Stefen was rapidly losing control.

"Keep him calm."

"Are the explosives set?"

"Yes. It's almost time."

"Somebody, hold him down."

Stefen abruptly stood, in full panic, and two of the musicians tried to force him back down on the bench. Stefen looked around himself. This wasn't what he had intended. A bomb! He had just wanted to get even with Gustof, and now all of this. He threw his bongos to one side and started to run.

~ ~ ~ ~ ~

Back in the Commanders office the four of them were staring at the video feeds from the park. A tall blonde man with a full beard, where was he? It was Gustof who spotted him first, sitting on a bench as a musician handed him a set of Bongos.

"That's him, there!" Gustof shouted, "Where the other musicians are heading to."

The Commander didn't hesitate to give his orders to the security details covering the park.

"We have them, southeast corner, memorial bench 14. We have them all. Move in quickly."

~ ~ ~ ~ ~

There were almost twenty members of the Cabal around Stefen as he broke away. They tried to tackle him, to hold him down, but that only brought more attention to the Cabal. They could all see clearly the security units moving in on them.

"It's them," Stefen screamed as he ran, pointing at the Cabal members he ran from.

"They have bombs," he shouted at the crowd of onlookers around him.

On hearing bomb the crowd around him began to run away quickly in a panic, leaving Stefen isolated on the park grounds. The crowd carried with the cry, "A bomb, a bomb!"

The leader of the Cabal now looked around at the others. He could see what was happening. In his twisted mind they could still pull this off and get away.

"Who has the detonator?" he asked the group around him.

"I do," a woman answered.

"The bombs," he cried out. "Detonate them."

"There are too many people around. They'll all die."

"Just do it."

"I can't," said the woman holding the detonator and she tossed it away from them, about fifteen feet away. She then turned and ran to the security personnel closing in.

"He has the detonator. He'll set it off."

The security forces quickly collected her and approached the others. More now moved away from the Cabal's leader, surrendering to the security teams. The Cabal's leader now looked around him, anxiously. He could still pull his won victory from this. The detonator was within reach. He would set it off himself. He popped a pill into his mouth. The drug would give him the courage he needed and he walked over to where the detonator lay on the ground. In his drug induced state, he heard the security forces order him not to move. It didn't matter, in his mind they wouldn't shoot, at least not until he set off the explosives.

Stefen had stopped 50 feet or so from the others. He had only wanted to punish Gustof for getting the grant that should have been his. What had he done? Who were these people that had recruited him?

"What did they do to me? What have I done?" Stefen called out aloud to nobody and everybody around him.

Stefen stood still, his gun now held in one hand, as he watched the Cabal's leader pick up the detonator. The two of them locked eyes for a moment. Stefen knew the security units wouldn't fire first; it wasn't in them. Stefen could see the vacant look in the mans eyes as he held the bombs trigger. He would set off the bombs before the security reached him. Stefen looked at the Cabal leader one more time and raised the gun he carried. The Cabal meant it for Gustof and Anya, but he had always known that he couldn't pull the gun's trigger on them. Now he knew he could pull the trigger. He had trained at the shooting ranges for this. Two shots, that was all he needed; two shots.

Stefen looked one last time at the Cabal leader, his hand holding the bombs trigger. The head of the Cabal just looked at Stefen in disbelief as the bullets struck his forehead and heart and he crumpled to the ground, the detonator falling harmlessly to one side.

After firing the shots, Stefen dropped the gun to the ground and fell to his knees.

"I am sorry," he said as he looked around him.

Around Stefen and the fallen Cabal leader, the remaining members of the Cabal who hadn't surrendered lay down their few weapons they carried, lay prostrate on the ground, and surrendered themselves to the security forces.

~ ~ ~ ~ ~

As Gustof, Anya, the Commander and Ashe watched the final scenes unfold on the video screens in the Commanders office, a crowd gathered around Stefen and the fallen Cabal leader. Ambulances arrived but nothing could be done for the Cabal's leader.

The four of them just sat down and looked at each other. It was over. The question in each of their minds was Stefen. In the end, was he a victim of his own hate or a hero, a savior in the end, bringing down the Cabal? Or was it as Gustof thought, a little of both.

~ ~ ~ ~ ~

It was two weeks later and Anya and Gustof were finally cleared from their isolation in the Security offices. They had met briefly with head of the Space Exploration Guild, Susan Bayfield and the Guild's Security Commander, Carl Skarieber. Decisions were being made, just not yet finalized; how to bring the news of Anya's discoveries to the world.

The Cabal had been contained, although they knew that there were still members out there, including in the Guild's own offices. Gustof and Anya were part of the interrogation of Stefen. They sat down in the interrogation room across from him. Neither of them recognized Stefen from the man they had known. He was clean shaven, but just carried a vacant stare in his eyes. Anya could see the tormented man that he had become, filled with sorrow and guilt.

Gustof and Stefen just stared at each other for the longest time, neither of them speaking a word. Gustof could see in Stefen's vacant eyes; nothing.

Finally Gustof leaned forward towards Stefen and asked him a single question.

"Why?"

Stefen tried to move in a nervous way, his hands spread wide in front of him, his head leaning forward, his eyes unfocused, in voice so low it could barely be heard.

"I should have won that grant. It was mine."

Gustof just looked over at Stefen incredulously and didn't say a word for a couple of minutes. Finally he stood up, took Anya's hand and replied to Stefen.

"That's what this was all about, the grant?"

Stefen looked up at the two of them standing before them and quietly nodded.

"Yes."

Gustof and Anya looked back and forth at each other, and then back at Stefen. As they reached the door to leave, Gustof looked back at Stefen one last time.

"I forgive you," Gustof said to his adversary through all of this.

Anya just gave a final uncompromising look at Stefen and the two of them walked out the door and left.

~ ~ ~ ~ ~

There was a new feeling of anxiety among the people of Earth and its colonies that had spread in the short time the Cabal had to spread its rumors and innuendo about just who and what Anya had found.

As Anya and Gustof left the Security Center that had been their home during the crisis, they were informed that an official announcement would be made in two weeks. It would be done, not from the Guild's Headquarters, but from Gustof and Anya's farm.

However the pair had other things to do first; a visit to Sulligan, now recovering from his head wound and surgery in his Guild apartment, and finally some time on the farm, just the two of them and the dogs.

Epilogue

Rumors had spread throughout Earth and the colonies and with those rumors spread even more stories, real and imagined, of the contact with the alien race.

News crews gathered to capacity in the driveway and in front of the porch of Gustof and Anya's farmhouse. Both the head of the Explorer's Guild and the Humanities Guild were inside the home with Anya and Gustof. The farmhouse was chosen as the setting of the formal announcement of the contact with another race as a way to calm Earth's population.

After several hours of waiting, Gustof, Anya and Mark Sulligan came out onto the porch and sat down in waiting chairs, Earths leaders standing behind them. In the end the Explorer's Guild and other Guild leaders decided it would be up to Anya what to say to the people of Earth and the colonies. Anya had insisted that Gustof be there at her side.

A podium was placed at the front of the porch and Susan Bayfield, the elected head of the Explorer's Guild and the de facto head of Earth and its colonies stood behind it.

So much had changed in the two months since Anya's return from her First Landing expedition. Already new measures were being put into place regarding future First Landings, exploration and colonies. The outward expansion of Earth would not be slowed, however new security measures were being developed and put into place.

"'Ladies and Gentlemen of our world, members of our colonies: explorers, seekers, builders, farmers, colonist and all of humanity, I speak directly to you now of our stars, our planets and of the future.

"Here we assemble at the farm of Senior Explorer Anya Tyszko and her Husband Gustof Tyszko, a leader in his own right of our agricultural development for our colonies.

"You all know of Anya and the rumors of her discoveries. I introduce you now to Anya, her apprentice on her remarkable journey, Mark Sulligan, and finally her husband Gustof.

At that the speaker, Susan Bayfield, sat down. The three she introduced now rose up from their seats and approached the podium with its mics and cameras; Anya, flanked on one side by Gustof and the other side by Sulligan. They stood quietly, side by side as one, as applause filled the air from the crowd assembled in front of them. Gustof and Anya, looking out over the crowd, could see their friends standing in the very front; Michael, Amanda, Phillip, Mark, Jack and Lilly, and their newest friend, Ashe.

Anya raised her hands into the air, holding the hands of Gustof and Sulligan as well, raising them all into the air. Anya looked over the crowd; there must have been thousands perched in front of them. Anya looked over at Gustof and smiled.

As the applause settled down Anya moved close to the podium in front of her. Speaking to a crowd like this wasn't her forte, but she had Gustof and Sulligan behind her, encouraging her to speak. The crowd, the earth and the colonies waited for her words with anticipation, waiting for confirmation of what Anya and Sulligan had discovered.

As the crowd in front of her quieted, awaiting her words, Anya finally spoke. Anya, with Gustof and Sulligan, had worked for hours on what to say. At first Susan Bayfield had wanted a long, elegant speech. In the end it was Gustof thoughts that carried the day. The words were simple, brief and direct.

"We step forward into a new place in the universe. We will continue to move forward and outward. However, we now know, we are not alone in this universe. And we head out now to find new friends and trading partners in our explorations. Thank-you."

www.ingramcontent.com/pod-product-compliance
Lightning Source LLC
LaVergne TN
LVHW010223070526
838199LV00062B/4701